graveyards, bars, and a graveyard bar

jerry purdon

Edited by
lisa lee tone

Cover Art
lisa vasquez

ISBN: 979-8-218-70377-6

TheJerryPurdon@gmail.com

For Krystal

introduction

Are you a fan of great complex stories with a tinge of horror, love, mystery, and the taste of mythology? Then this is the place for you.

A gifted storyteller, Jerry spends hours perfecting his craft, always looking for a better way to tell a story. He is constantly looking for new ways to grab the reader into the depths of the tale and make her not want to leave it.

This short collection will give you a wonderful taste of the breadth of Jerry's talents, making you crave even more.

Don't worry you'll get even more, so dive in and savor these pages and revel as each story brings a new reveal, a new twist, and a more satisfying ending.

- Lisa Diane Kastner

graveyard game

. . .

A COOL LATE AUTUMN BREEZE RUSTLED THE LEAVES AT LISA'S FEET AS she stood before the open cemetery gate. Chills settled along her neck and shoulders as her skin pimpled. Lisa's gaze centered on the hulking tree in the middle of the graveyard. Its massive bare branches stretched out across the landscape with limbs like huge extremities waiting to pluck anyone who dared to enter.

"It's not quite everything," Tommy said.

"Then why do I have to do it?"

"There's nothing to it. All you have to do is walk in, go past the oak, stab a grave, and run out." He made a quick hand gesture as he stabbed down at the air, then moved his arms as if running. A mischievous smile followed his mimed actions. "And when I say run out, I really mean get the hell out of there."

Lisa focused on the gleam of his blue eyes. The late afternoon breeze blowing in their faces made him squint ever so slightly, allowing him to appear as if he posed for an action photo. This caused her only a minor distraction as she searched the deep recesses of her mind for any plausible excuse.

"Why can't I wait until summer when the others go?" she asked with a tilt of her head, inciting her bangs to slide down her forehead.

Her dark shoulder-length hair followed with a shift across the collar of her denim jacket.

"Because you're already in the eighth grade, which makes you well past the seventh, which is the year everyone does it. Any new kid our age or older must make The Run alone."

"Even if I were a senior?"

"If you wanted a date to the prom."

Lisa rolled her eyes. When she first learned about "The Run," she believed it all belonged in the category of a simple prank for the new kid. Soon after, she realized how deep this tradition went in the small town of three thousand. At this point, she wished she'd failed the sixth grade twice. She did not want to mill around any graveyard at midnight, including the one she visited now. Lisa weighed her options. She had no choice. She did not consider being ignored for the next four and a half school years as a viable option.

"I don't like that tree," she muttered.

"Wicked, ain't it?"

She jumped at the sound of a car horn before she could reply. An old green Chevy truck waited to pull onto the gravel drive where they stood. Above a hideous rust hole in the bottom of the door was Nessler's Lawn Care in faded yellow print and the phone number, dulled under the mixture of neglect and dirt. An unfriendly white-whiskered face peered through the half-opened cab window. His gray eyes pierced through the two young teens.

"Y'all gonna move, or do I get to flatten ya?"

His coarse voice ran like fingernails across a chalkboard in Lisa's ears.

"Come on." Tommy tugged on her jacket sleeve. "I'll walk you home."

As they walked away, the truck rolled to the front gate and the driver got out.

"Hey!" the old man yelled.

His gruff sound followed them along the sidewalk. They quickened their pace.

"You stop when I'm talkin' to ya!"

Tommy froze and kept his face forward. Lisa followed her new friend's lead.

"Nights are longer now. Don't wanna see any of you kids hangin' around here. If I catch ya playin' games here, I'll skin your hides. Hear me? You HEAR me? You got your own pissant yards. Now scat!"

Lisa trailed Tommy to the street corner, where he stopped.

"Get ready," Tommy whispered and turned toward the old man locking the gate. The chain clanged against the iron. "Hey, Old Man! Blow it out your ASS!"

They ran for a few short blocks to the plain two-story house where she lived. In the front yard, her father bagged the last pile of leaves. Both kids slowed to a trot.

"Hiya, Dad."

"Hi, Lisa. Tommy."

"Hi, Mr. Collins."

"Don't you mean blow it out your ass?" Lisa mumbled.

Tommy stiffened.

"What's so funny, hon?"

"Nothing, Dad. I'm just giving Tommy a bad time."

"Oh." He smiled. "About the ol' Eddie Haskell routine?"

"The what? Who's Eddie Hassle?"

"Haskell, we've seen that show together … never mind."

"I love doing that to him," she murmured to Tommy.

Mr. Collins went to the side of the house, and the two adolescents said their good-byes. Lisa waited for Tommy to kiss her as she hoped for him to do for the past two weeks, but he shuffled his feet too many times. After his head ducked, no hope existed for their first time no matter how far she leaned forward.

After her classmate left, Lisa continued her evening routine. She ate supper and dodged questions on all things Tommy. She finished her homework, followed by a touch of television before retiring to bed. The only difference for her on this night centered on her night-wear. She ditched her flannel nightshirt pajamas for dark jeans and a blouse, something she wore for switching out stage sets at her old school's theatre. Lisa placed the black tennis shoes at her bedside, and a baseball cap resided by her window. Her escort for the main event, Tommy, said to meet him across the street at midnight.

She tried to sleep, but her anxieties kept her wide awake. Her mind rampaged on all the past stories she'd heard. Especially about the girl who died during a grave stabbing journey. It made no sense for a healthy teenager to die of a heart attack from being scared. Probably some unknown birth defect. When Lisa searched the internet, the first answer to her search returned as affirmative for a death scare. Another reason not to believe the web, and definitely on the first thing that popped up. So she stopped her exploration. Besides, the girl's death struck Lisa as a little too convenient, and she surmised no one ever wound up dead. The tale, passed from older siblings to younger siblings, grew over time and went from what actually happened to now a currently deceased girl. If true, then a definite unknown heart condition. Lisa wondered about her possible conditions. A sense of dread came over her as the minutes counted down toward her assigned time to rise.

Of course, the dead girl stories centered on her beauty and how no one went to save her when she screamed. Everyone ran from the cemetery. The next day, someone found her in the graveyard with one foot stuck in a grave like something tried to pull her down into a crypt. The whole nonsense came down to some made-up fish fable, and it shrieked of major bullshit.

Lisa construed the situation as quite odd, since no one recalled the girl's name. Browsing old newspapers through something called microfiche in their school library yielded no results. Their librarian complained they didn't have the budget to have everything converted to digital copies. Lisa related to the statement because she didn't have the funds for a new iPad, which would upgrade her sad excuse for a laptop. Searches online produced nothing, and she couldn't ask her parents or another adult because word would be out the kids planned another night of teenage hazing pranks at the old town graveyard.

The only other story of legendary status centered on a boy named Samuel Brown. Old Man Nessler apparently bailed him out of trouble. The only problem with Sam, he never spoke about it. No one ever learned what happened other than to say that Nessler probably played a trick on him. Tommy speculated the two cut a deal so the sly old fellow could continue to terrorize any poor soul who dared to enter after dark.

In both stories, the unfortunate students performed their cemetery night exercise all alone, and the prominent setup reeked of a "let's terrify the new kid" kind of prank. All of the summertime versions for when the whole class went as a group only told fun tales about kids running into one another, someone accidentally cutting themselves, or a boyfriend and girlfriend making out over a grave. Those were the cool ones. Not her; she found herself alone and going during late fall, the darkest time of year. Scream Queens became a thing for her since this setup started like a horror movie. The inclusion process of wanting to belong and having to handle the gauntlet of teenage peer pressure from such a small group convinced her she lacked the power to say no. As her grandmother always told her, "No is a complete sentence." Lisa regretted lacking the guts to convey the one word.

According to Tommy, the decision for "The Run" always happened at the last second. This helped to keep their event from being discovered by adults. Nobody's parents would go for it, especially in the dead of the night. She completely understood her parents' perspective; those hours belonged to witches, bloodsuckers, drug dealers, carjackers, and young lovers waiting to be mutilated.

Her barely audible phone buzz came alive at midnight but loud enough to make her jump. Her cue to rise finally alerted her. With a slight hesitation, she reset her alarm for school and put her feet on the floor. Lisa took an extra pillow from underneath her bed to create her shadowy under-cover body double. Her parents never attempted opening her locked door. They did not believe in violating her private space, so the need for the additional stuff in the sheets disguise came from her being-prepared-for-anything mentality. Her personal motto centered around: one can never assume when it comes to parents.

She took a quick pause by her mirror within the glow of outside night lights to primp her hair and apply a dash of lip gloss before cracking open the window and slipping out. Behind her, teenage influences stared from their various locked-in-time positions on her wall. She mused about their jealousy of her freedom as she sat on the windowsill. With a wink, she waved bye and headed out.

The second story elevation did not pose a problem for her. A ledge between the two stories jutted out about two inches further than the tip of her shoes. From this point, the ground was only ten feet below. She jumped, landing with a sudden thump, and rolled into the forward motion. At that moment, Lisa loved her father a ton more than ever since he'd raked the leaves earlier that evening. It would have taken her an hour to remove them all out of her hair and clothes.

Lisa scrambled to stand and straightened her cap. Tommy stepped from behind an aged maple tree and almost caused her to scream. She remained calm. She didn't think he caught her startled jump.

"Did you move the ladder to the side of the house?"

"Relax, Lisa. Everything's cool."

"You sure?"

"It's right over there."

He motioned in the dark, but she couldn't see where he pointed.

"We'd better go," Tommy said as he grabbed her arm and ran.

They trotted along the sidewalk, staying out of the light of a street lamp. Only twice did they veer from the complete coverage of trees that stood in manicured lawns. They walked once they reached the corner. Lisa thought about how much of a disadvantage it was to live so close to a boneyard.

"Are you ready?"

"I hope so."

"Scared?"

"The pee-my-pants kind."

"I would pee my pants if I went into a graveyard by myself in the middle of the night."

"Tommy! Stop it."

"Oh, come on. It's no big deal."

"So why do it?"

"Because we all do. Besides, you don't want the dweeb label."

"Is that all?"

"No, I'd stick around."

His faint smile shimmered in the lamplight, and the white of his teeth glowed. She memorized his sly expression from the first day she met him, and butterflies bloomed in her since.

"Well, let's get the ladder, and I'll go back to bed."

"I'm not letting you chicken out. If you need me, just scream, and I'll be in there before you know it."

His words comforted her, though the thought to create the highest pitched shriek any human ever conjured up to unhinge her classmates propagated throughout her psyche. Being absolutely terrified in doing this stupid tradition made it easy to expel as much air as possible, and if she freaked anyone out, then bonus. Her mind eased a bit knowing of her own joke she planned for the others making her participate in this early teenage hazing.

Before more thoughts of what she could do to make the night memorable caught her attention, they reached the cemetery. Her heart picked up its pace.

"We need to cross the road at an angle. We don't need to get in that light." He pointed to another street lamp.

When they arrived at the gates, other kids were there. Except she saw no smiles. There were a few remarks of "good luck" from those who were familiar from her classes and the hall.

One girl, Denise Johnson, who seemed to be the most popular in the school, patted Lisa on the back and congratulated her for showing up. Lisa caught an occasional sparkle of their eyes, but the dark kept the faces shadowed. The solemn mood of the crowd bothered her.

"Do you have a knife?" somebody asked.

"Oh crap, I didn't know I was supposed to bring one."

"What in the hell did you think you were going to stab the grave with?"

"Tommy didn't mention it."

"They're only picking," Tommy stated.

A few soft chuckles erupted. She relaxed a bit, realizing everyone played their part in an attempt to freak her out a little more. *It's all a game,* she thought. One eligible for her to play at too.

"Here."

Tommy handed her the cutter, but it felt like a sword in her hand.

"What kind of knife is this?"

"Hanson's old man is a butcher. It's one of his knives."

"Oh."

"Be sure to bring it back with you," Hanson reminded.

Lisa went to the brick wall to the right of the gate. Placing her hands on the flat brick coping, she lifted herself up. She rested facing the street. Tommy grabbed her hand.

"You remember the rules?"

Lisa nodded. She thought she understood all of the rules.

"These are important. I'm going over them one more time. You have to go past the oak where the drive splits. Then you can stick any grave after that point. You'll be in the center of the graveyard. Once done, you haul ass back."

"With the knife," Hanson added.

"Got it. Anything else?" Lisa glanced around to see if she was actually supposed to go through with the ridiculous activity. The whole thing was stupid. She should somehow make it fun. Hopefully, she could think of something besides screaming.

"You're free to go anytime you want," Tommy said.

"See ya."

Lisa swung her legs over and jumped down. She trotted over to the gravel path and jogged toward the oak.

"Wouldn't wanna be ya," Hanson said.

His voice carried, and Lisa caught his every word. She kept the butcher sword forward, mainly to keep from cutting herself. Her nerves tapped on the edge of frenzy, but she steadied them as she braced her foremost thoughts about how other kids might jump out at her.

Her vision picked up the faint white pebbles of the drive beneath her feet. The headstones along either side of her glowed in the moonlight like individual beacons, each an island with their own lighthouse guiding her through the dangerous waters to the shore ahead. She maintained a focus for the oak tree, where her present trail eventually split. Without any street lighting in the graveyard, her eyes adjusted completely to the night as she kept her heading to her first goal. Though the farther she went from the gate, the more she felt like someone in a post-apocalyptic universe trudging through a wrecked environment by themself.

Of course, noises abounded everywhere. She found it odd how vision dimmed in the dark but the ears became supersonic sensitive to any sound, real or imagined. Hoots from an owl up ahead and the rustling of tree limbs from the breeze. In the distance, a dog barked far away from this particular necropolis. The crack of a twig snapping caused her to gasp. She hoped the wind created that ruckus; however, she prepared herself for there to be others hiding behind the enormous headstones, waiting for their chance to terrorize her. An explanation existed for every major and minor clamor. Of course, she lacked the knowledge of what those might be, at least in most cases.

Her inner dialogue mumbled this was all normal cemetery nightlife. Though her imagination plagued her with corpses rising from the grave and poltergeists ascending up for revenge on the breathing. She forced her mind to picture something else, like maybe squirrels playing in the dark. Lisa worked on imagining nature over zombies.

Distinguishing any noises coming from the other side of the brick wall proved impossible for her. All she heard were the surrounding constants. Another twig or two breaking. The constant of the barn owl in a tree ahead of her, as well as the leaves rustling on the ground around her as her own shoes crunched the gravel beneath her feet.

Football fields were not foreign to her since her involvement with the school band. From where she stood, the iron gate was more than a hundred yards, definitely more than the length of the gridiron. Nonetheless, for her, it might as well have been miles away. She did not see anyone behind her, or, for that matter, where she started from; it now blended in the dark. Lisa turned forward and continued her trek toward the mammoth oak hulking over where the path split. Massive branches reached out to every point of the expansive yard. Of course, the science part of her brain reasoned on the impossibilities of the limbs being able to pluck someone up from anywhere on the grave-yard grounds, but it appeared to have the capability, causing her more concern than she originally thought. In fact, the old tree manifested itself larger than when she stared at it earlier that afternoon.

"How did you get so big," she said in the direction of the hardwood.

Finally, her feet cusped the edge of the drive where it split east and west. Two graves separated her and the oak, they loomed as sentries waiting to move and drag her underneath the soil. She walked between the headstones toward the other side of the massive trunk. Lisa stepped over several roots jutting above ground. She thought they were like the branches overhead, stretching to every corner of the cemetery, piercing through the older coffins, allowing things to infiltrate and feast on what lay within. She shuddered. The awareness that whatever could enter a grave created the path for something to exit gained traction. She shook her head, attempting to clear her mind and refocus on the task at hand.

Lisa reached the other side of the tree. Nothing happened. A wave of disappointment washed over her without the explosion of ghosts or fellow teenagers rushing out at her. Instead, scattered headstones greeted her with their carved lettering of long forgotten names.

"I'm only killing dirt," she said with a sigh.

She stepped forward to the nearest grave. All of a sudden, the knife became heavy in her hand. From behind her, she thought something stirred. Lisa quickly turned. Peripherally, a white dress fluttered. As she stared in the direction, only the dark allowed for her full view; nothing else was there.

She smiled with the understanding someone would eventually step up and say "boo" as soon as she struck the ground. Either her class-mates or the old spook Nessler himself. She hoped for the students. She fully expected to face the same prank as Samuel.

"Losers," she said and knelt next to a gravesite. The light hairs on her neck and arms bristled. In her mind, warning bells went off, and a sudden dread came over her.

"How else would they know," she asked herself as she gripped the knife in her hand, "unless they lurked from the shadows?" Hence the disturbing feeling within her; somewhere, others hid nearby. It was the only way they would ever find out. She explained away her inner alarm and the feel of something peering over her, waiting.

"No offense," she croaked as if to coax the earth beneath her feet.

Lisa raised the knife high, as far as her arm stretched. The brandished blade reflected no light. Warnings continued through a vigorous internal shriek and filled her soul with such an uneasiness she became nauseous. A cool breeze whispered in her ear.

"What?" she asked, and her immediate tremble physically displayed her angst.

Lisa swallowed in an effort to control her fear. If she did not gain power over herself, her imagination would definitely rule over everything she did. Noises in the wind would have to blow by her. She steeled her soul and stretched the knife to the sky one more time. Obviously, other kids were nearby watching her every move. Once she sliced through the ground, they would jump out. Probably from the other side of the oak. Again, she thought she saw a flash of white clothing from behind the trunk.

"Oh, screw it," Lisa grumbled.

She extended her hand high, ready to plunge the butcher tool in the grave next to where she knelt. She breathed in as much as possible. Her lungs ready to burst. The planned scream prepared as soon as she plunged the steel into earth. A chill ran across the back of her neck. In a solid downward motion, she flung her arm full force, easily thrusting the knife hilt deep into the dirt. Right after the tip of the blade touched dry earth, the air around her became ice cold. Something grasped her shoulder.

Lisa exhaled through her howl. Though she may have prepped for it, her jolted vocal chords stung as her genuine shriek continued. She struggled to stand. The strong hand held her in place. She let go another screech.

"Shut up, missy."

A slight slap from the back of a hand tapped the back of her head. She recognized the gruff voice. Busted. A different type of dread enveloped her down to her gut. Lisa's urge to go home evaporated.

"You shouldn't be playin' games this time of night! You could get hurt real bad."

She stayed put with her head ducked. Tears welled in her eyes.

"Come on. My truck is by the back gate."

The old man extended his hand. She grasped it and stood. His hand felt like ice, and the chilled air hit her face like a splash of water waking her from a dream.

"Why is it so cold?"

"You always ask this many questions?"

"It was just one."

"And that's too damned many. You kids are a bunch of wiseacres, anyway. You always know what's best. Besides, I already said to come on, and time's a wastin'."

She followed the old man. He seemed dull and moved slow, as if concentrating to keep each step in the rightful place. Any glimpse of light faded away on him. His steps carried them past the oak tree.

Something brushed across the back of her neck. The wind weakened, and the breeze whispered again. Lisa turned, and again, nothing was there. Cold surrounded her and embraced her almost as if it were a hug.

"Cemeteries play tricks like that. Ignore them."

"I don't like it."

"Well, missy, that's just too damn bad!"

She got the idea maybe the mean in him sucked all of his color out.

The air softened, and this time, the message was clear: *"Don't follow him."*

"What was that?" she asked.

"Kelly, you leave us alone. You hear?"

"Who's Kelly?"

"Never you mind. Now let's go."

The breeze brushed by her again: *"Don't go; help is coming."*

Lisa looked toward the old man. His eyes lacked a sparkle. There was no flash in the moonlight. The orbs appeared dull and empty. Fear flooded every part of her body.

"I'm not going."

"Yes, you are, missy!"

He grabbed her shoulder, and Lisa collapsed. The old man wasted no time. He bent over, seized an ankle, and started dragging her along the ground. He pulled her with minimal effort or concern for what bumped her head. She tried to plant her free foot, kick at him, or grab a shrub. Nothing helped her. The dirt loosened, making it easier for her to slip along.

"STOP IT!"

The old man chuckled as he continued forward. Her words gave the man no pause. Lisa screamed again, as loud as she could, and was inhaling again when she felt another cool, gentle breeze across her face.

"Help is coming."

She relaxed.

"Kelly, now, leave us be." The old man grunted the last word. "You're not talkin' about that boy, are you?"

There was no response, almost as if they were left alone.

"About time you learnt your place," he shouted to the air. He smiled and turned back to Lisa. "And about time you learnt yours."

Lisa tried to jerk her leg back, but her efforts brought nothing but a tightened grip. The cold from his fingers ran up her calf, numbing everything below her knee. She yanked once more, and he tugged with more might.

"That's all you got, missy?"

She closed her eyes for a few seconds. Something like a cloth crossed her face. She attempted to sit up but became entangled in white material. She thought it might be a dress.

"Kelly, I said stay out of this."

"Let go of her, you old ghost."

Lisa moved her head to uncover her face. Still, fabric shielded her eyes. Her hands clawed into the soil. She attempted to grab on to anything in case the old man started dragging her again. Each time she shifted her head, the garment remained bunched over her eyes. A flash brightened through the cloth.

"Kelly, I ain't amused. Now PISS OFF!"

"I don't think so. Let go."

The words floated in and out of Lisa's head. Kelly's sounds were like musical notes, except the last note vibrated from the final chord. There was another shimmer, and her ankle freed.

"Someone else is coming, and now, it's either her or the boy. Make up your mind, Kelly."

"Your brother is almost here."

The brisk air surrounding them became more frigid. It reminded her of how everything chilled right before a snowfall. No wind existed. Only the cold. Ice crystalized on the ground around her.

"I'll get him, then."

With the old man's words, another flare crisped the night. This one lacked the brightness of the others. The dress vanished above her. Free, Lisa sat up. As her eyes adjusted from the sudden bursts, in the dull moonlight, she saw nothing.

The freeze dissipated, but everything remained cool. She stood up and went toward the oak. Lisa understood that after she rediscovered the gravel path, she would have found her way out.

She ignored the questions forming in her head. Like who was the boy and who pulled her? What brother? Lisa needed a plan for leaving as fast as she could.

She arrived at the tree and picked up on an irritated male's voice. A sudden realization hit; those vocals didn't belong to Nessler.

"He's mine," the hard, angry man said.

"No, he's only knocked out," a woman responded.

A beam of light whitened the area ahead of her, not as bright as the flash but steady like car headlights. She assumed they were from Nessler's truck. He must have pulled up with the vehicle lining up to the left of the main gate.

In that glow, she saw someone laid out on the ground with two figures standing over them. Lisa easily identified the faded old man, and she strained her vision, determining the other was the person in white.

"Carl, you leave that boy alone."

Nessler approached and stood in his truck's luminescence.

"Stay out of this, little brother."

"You ceased being my brother when you became a haunt. Now scat, or I'll be back with Father Paul."

"That old battle axe back in town?"

"He is."

The pale ghost dissipated. The white-dressed girl turned to look in Lisa's direction and waved good-bye. In a mere moment, only Nessler and the crumpled body on the ground were left.

"Come over here," Nessler said.

She ran toward Nessler and stopped short of him with a slow walk. Her eyes focused on Tommy lying on the path. A noticeable gash centered on his forehead. Nessler lifted Tommy without a strain. They both walked to his truck.

"What's your name?" Nessler asked.

"Lisa."

"Okay, Lisa, we'll leave for the Doc's from here. After we get there, we'll need to call your parents."

She didn't say a word and opened the door, allowing Nessler to place Tommy in the middle of the bench seat.

"Come on, get in."

She climbed in and settled herself as he laid Tommy near her, the boy's head in her lap. She could see blood matted to the part in his hair. Lisa only wanted him to wake up and smile. Tears welled in her eyes.

"Don't worry, Tommy will be fine. He's just a bit dazed. Did ya yell or somethin'?"

Confused, she stared at the old man.

"Did ya scream when the yard went cold?"

"Yes, sir."

"You're more pleasant when usin' manners and not phrases about what I can do with my backside."

The old man kept his eyes on the road. The glare from the dashboard reflected in the old man's eyes. This old man was definitely among the living. She even saw his faint smile. Knowing what Tommy said earlier and now the old man saving them, she wanted to melt into oblivion.

"Tommy must like ya a lot," the old man commented.

"Really?"

"Yeah, he's grown up here and knows the past pretty well. Most likely didn't ever believe the stories, but on your screamin', he went to help. Being aware of all those tales and runnin' beyond that gate took some courage. And every bit of those tales are true."

"He knew about the ghosts?"

"Nah, that's you seein' things. Still, you stay out of the yard at night, especially this time of year."

"Kelly wasn't my imagination."

"She sure wasn't, but keep her there. She was a smidge older than you when she died in that place. Don't mention anything about seeing her, and people 'round here will leave you be, yet if you yap about it, people won't like it. That could get perty bad. Again, it's best to stay out of that yard."

"Yes, sir."

"You'll be a part of those stories now. Just like Samuel. Just like Kelly, though no one ever mentions her name. That's a sad thing. Even the newspaper didn't touch her event back in the day."

Lisa nodded. Nessler told the truth; she fathomed that much. She tried to look beyond the headlights on the road ahead, but Kelly entered her mind. She wanted to ask Nessler questions about the person who fought for her and against his older brother but decided to leave it alone.

She only rode a few miles, but the ride took forever. Once her parents found out about tonight, she would be grounded until she left for college. Her room would definitely be checked each night. Prior to graduating high school, they would watch her every move. Suddenly, she remembered the knife. Lisa realized that more than her and Tommy were receiving punishments. She sighed.

"Stupid small-town traditions."

ghosts in the graveyard

. . .

"LET'S PLAY," COLIN SAID AS HE TOSSED A CASUAL NOD TOWARD THE cemetery.

Cassie's doe-eyed shock shuddered through her body in an instant, followed by an intense heat from deep within. It radiated up through her chest, neck, and face. She hated him for the mere suggestion of the game and hoped her cheeks had not become too visible to everyone. She knew her reddened state probably appeared brighter against the backdrop of the blue jersey she wore. Her eyes tightened as she delivered a cold stare right at his soul and silently prayed for his brain to hemorrhage.

Over the summer, she'd told him her secret. She confided in him. Trusted him. Now, she realized he either didn't care or didn't believe her. Possibly both. So much for whatever they had.

"Halloween is over. Cemeteries aren't fun now," Cassie said. Her flat tone almost carried a mother's weight to it. With one brow propped up, she wanted someone to agree with her. As she waited for a concurrence, she imagined her betrayer grabbing his head with blood spurting from his nose and collapsing to the ground.

THE YEAR BEFORE, she walked alone. The fading light of dusk hit early due to the clouds as well as the hardwoods still having most of their leaves. The air seemed cooler as it touched her face, giving her a crisp, refreshed feeling. It lured her to go further and deeper to the back.

It was Monday, not her usual Wednesday church youth crowd. Her mom came to help with some Christmas project. Cassie lucked out when she finished her assigned chore and then asked to go out for a walk. She barely contained her excitement when granted permission.

She journeyed across the tar covered road, through the chain-link gate, and onto the white gravel hearse path, where the luminescence created a shallow glow.

She had no idea why she walked to the back of the cemetery by herself in the paling light and straight for the broken fence. Once at the maple tree, she peered down the slope through the wooded area toward the creek bed. It was dark. An owl glided into the obscurity of the trees, only to perch on an unseen limb and look back at her with moonlit eyes. She wished she had her phone for a picture, but the old country church had no cell towers anywhere near it, so she'd left it in the car.

A flash down by the creek caught her attention. Perhaps a hunter walked along the water with a flashlight. She hiked further away from the tree and closer to the bottom before seeing more than one shimmer, which gave her pause. Small lit spheres appeared and were something she never experienced before. The tiny balls wove in and out of the trees as well as shooting up above the forest. They reminded her of birds chasing one another, no different from their own game of ghosts.

Except one of the orbs broke away and headed straight for her. It stopped about halfway between the creek and where she stood. The sphere never moved closer. She was glad since her legs and feet acted as if they were encased in concrete.

The white light mesmerized her. Intermittent bands of yellow and orange streaked across the exterior. The colored flicks occasionally shot out from the surface, yet it stayed as frozen as she was for the moment.

She jumped when a voice spoke. The sound was in her head and nothing like her own inner voice. No, this one held a deep, feminine tone along with a predominate rasp. The intonation reminded her of how her great-grandmother sounded. How she spoke while hooked to oxygen tubes and still continuing a two-pack-a-day habit.

Though the inflection fascinated her, the question created goosebumps.

"Ever burn?"

She tried to think of some reason as to what was happening. Did this thing actually say something to her? Though it didn't come through her ears.

"Burn?" it asked.

She finally began to breathe and responded with shaking her head.

"You will," it said.

A cackle started and turned into a chortle to the point she expected a coughing fit to follow. Her head echoed the chuckle as it became a loud, hoarse, raucous laughter, and it yelled:

"You will!"

When the cemented sensation in her legs evaporated, she sprinted up the hill back to the church. Cassie did not appreciate being laughed at by some possessed bright ball of gas, though the thought of something like this speaking to her freaked her out. There was no way this thing knew about her. Somehow, she must have hallucinated, but it didn't feel that way. She couldn't think of a way to bring it up to her mom, but she did some web research. Of course, she found plenty of descriptions about will-o'-the-wisps, but nothing about voices. Every other site indicated the phenomenon was nothing more than a leaky gas pipe.

Cassie asked her dad, who reiterated the gas pipes spiel. She believed he knew she didn't like his response. Her pops spoke with Mr. Broussard, a church deacon who also served as the head of the Camp County Public Works.

Of course, his team found nothing, no leaky gas pipes, and didn't detect any lighted orbs since the fact-finding mission happened in the middle of the day. Brilliant.

THE SLOW, deliberate touch of a smaller hand wrapped around the warmth of hers brought her back from her searing hate-fueled fantasy. The contact gave her a clear signal Jimmy trusted her. He was her junior by four years, and yes, he could be a pain like all younger kids, except she adored her little cousin. Though he was small and did everything at the speed of a sloth, he managed to become something more endearing than a relative or friend. He was the little brother she always wanted.

"Oh, come on," Colin pleaded, "let's have some fun while they chat."

His thumb pointed toward the church, causing their collective heads to turn to look. The ongoing adult conversation would not end anytime soon. Cassie did have second thoughts about her earlier Colin prayer and how it may have been a tad harsh. Nonetheless, betrayal was something not to be ignored.

"Let's go," Sandy said.

In her reddened state, Cassie didn't come close to hiding her new surprise. She couldn't believe the mousy youth would ever jump at the chance to play this stupid game. This girl worried too much about her hair to get sweaty playing among tombstones. Now, Cassie regretted not confiding in her best friend. Maybe her buddy would have suggested something different. Neither Zane, Mark, Nick, nor Darlene offered an alternative.

So Colin took off running through the open cemetery gate. Cassie figured he headed to the back, where it would be getting dark by now. Their hiding spots existed far enough away to where the church lights were a mere glimmer like a distant star. He cut straight across the grass and graves. He didn't follow the car path and was almost halfway across the whole cemetery before Cassie took one step. She stared into the darkening landscape and wondered why there were no lamps in the graveyard.

"I got you," she said to Jimmy. "Just don't leave my side. We won't go past the fence."

Jimmy squeezed her hand as they walked, while the others followed Colin at their quickest jogs. Her cousin's slow, methodical approach to almost everything he undertook made whatever he did notably pronounced. To her, he only did one thing fast; the boy loved soccer.

She wondered if they shouldn't go back to leave him with their parents, but doing so would raise too much suspicion. Besides, her previous graveyard stint had to be some sort of demented hallucination. Despite that, deep within the pit of her stomach, she believed they headed for certain doom.

So their walk happened on Jimmy time. They stayed to the hearse path. Cassie liked how the moonlight illuminated the white rocks. How with each minute, the glow intensified as night grew.

The group all knew Jimmy and would fit him in once he got there. Cassie was in no hurry whatsoever. She relished their slow saunter and heard the faraway shouts of the others as they played their first round of ghosts, saw their presence silhouetted against the various dark shades. She savored the game's name even though it was nothing more than a label. It was really hide-and-seek except in an ominous setting. Everyone would hide behind a massive headstone or tree near the huge maple where the seeker counted down.

She enjoyed the woods and loved the outdoors, hiking, and camping. Her liking this area centered on how different it was from other parts of East Texas, since there were very few pines. The cemetery cozied right up to the edge of the small forest. Most of the trees were pecan or dogwoods, with plenty of cedar and ash mixed in, along with her all-time favorite: maples. She loved the palmate leaves and believed good luck came from holding them. As a result, she liked everything maple, from syrup to the cute blue jerseys of Toronto's hockey team. She had no idea about the city the jersey represented until she received one for her last birthday. Then she became astute to all things Toronto. She wanted to go, but so far, no planned vacation existed.

Though she loved maple, Cassie especially cherished the one they used as home base for their graveyard game. To her, the huge trunk and heavy limbs acted as a type of sentry for all the interred.

The other kids were nowhere to be seen. They must have been hiding, and the seeker near the oversized bole. So far, there was nothing like last year, but it still troubled her. She chose not to run off to the back because she hoped their parents would call for them before she ever reached their purlieu. She didn't want to relive any part of what she encountered last fall, and if anything did happen, then Colin deserved total retribution. Traitor.

Since she had seen the first flicker, none of them had been able to play after evening church while it was dark because it was either raining, too wet, or too cold. Until now.

Her hair fell into her view. She blew air upwards, let go of Jimmy's hand as she stopped to redo her clip. She turned to face her sidekick with her back to where their friends played. The younger boy stared at her. He offered the slightest of smiles to offset his otherwise blank expression. The random shouts of "missed me" and "almost," then "you're it" filled their ears.

They paused at the top of the last hill before the path descended to the maple tree. Dusk gave way to night. The white graveled glow hit the brightest it would be, as did the unstained portion of the marble tombstones.

"We'll walk past the remaining headstones as they finish this next round," she said. "Or maybe we'll get lucky and our parents will call us."

They were only about halfway along the path which would eventually turn and go down the back side of the cemetery. There would be two family plots between the broken fence and the crushed gravel. On the other side of the break would be the large maple.

Jimmy grabbed his ears as a high-pitch sound started and resonated like someone scratching their fingernails across a chalkboard slate. Cassie kept her focus on her companion and made a concerted effort not to flinch at the noise.

The playful screams dissipated, but something different came from

Sandy. It was more of a shriek but cut off almost as quick. No matter the length of time, it sounded like what Cassie would think of as sheer terror. She almost glanced over her shoulder, but Jimmy maintained her attention. Concerned, she was about to start escorting him back up the trail to the front of the graveyard when the darkness evaporated.

Cassie saw her own shadow containing the smaller boy. Complete silence followed, and the air stilled as the brightness faded. She realized she needed to pee as her cousin carefully peeked around her. She could clearly see his eyes as he stared out beyond her. They didn't change expression, didn't widen in shock or squint because of the recent luster. He turned his focus on her and ever so slightly shook his head.

A sudden rush of air carried a sweet and acrid scent that hit her senses like a tsunami. The jolt of it almost made her fall over. Her nose wrinkled, as did Jimmy's, and she fought the urge to gag.

Everything went black. Her eyes took a second to adjust.

"What the hell was that?" Donnie asked. His voice sounded like it was right next to her.

They now stood on the grass. With a quick glance around, she noticed the two family plots between her and the moonlit gravel path. Her spine tingled from the neck down. She had no idea how they'd moved. Jimmy's slow grasp of her hand gave her some comfort.

"Sandy?" Colin called out her name for her whereabouts, and Cassie thought she detected a twinge of worry.

Everyone else except Sandy stood off to Cassie's right. All of them stared toward their base. She realized it was where her best friend had last been seen.

"I don't think she's behind the tree," Darlene added.

"We have to go toward the crick." Zane pointed.

Several orbs of light came into Cassie's view. She wanted to turn and run away, but not with Jimmy at her side. Her chest tightened, and she brought her elbows into her side. She hoped to make herself as small as possible as she watched them dance down at the bottom of the slope where the water flowed underneath the thick covering of assorted trees. Most of the hardwoods' leaves had already fallen to the forest floor, so it was easy to spot any lights down at the creek.

"I think that's her," Nick said.

"She's not a light ball," Mark spat.

"No, dummy, she's right there." Nick took off past home base.

"Uh, dude," Mark responded with a slight pause. "You can't see in the dark." He followed after Nick.

Both boys reached Sandy with their phone flashlights on. They studied her and pointed at different areas. Nick turned to the others.

"Looks like she's been burned," he said.

Colin headed toward the guys, and the rest pursued him, except Cassie. She stood back and faced Jimmy. He had tears running down his cheeks.

"Go get our parents," she said. "Keep your eyes on the church lights. Head straight to them." His hand squeezed hers before he took off toward the white gravel path. As he ran past the first headstones, she bellowed, "Run soccer fast!"

She turned to the others. They stood around the girl. Cassie counted heads against the many flickers still down by the creek bed. She had all of them except Sandy and Jimmy. One should be headed away and bringing back parents. The other, well, she hoped would be okay.

Cassie stepped even with the maple to be closer to the group. She didn't want to go further. The wisp's words still haunted her. Her gang's heads were still dots in the distance. Their shadowy figures still blended against the darkening landscape, but she could hear more of the conversation. As any one phone lit up, contrasting against their surroundings, it somehow gave Cassie some hope for all of them.

"Looks like there are a lot of those balls of light down there," Nick said.

"Will-o'-the-wisp," Colin corrected.

"What?"

"Will-o'-the-wisp."

"How do you know?" Zane asked.

"Because Cassie told me about them last year." Colin stared back at

Cassie. She could see the glisten in his eyes from all the phone flashlights.

"Well, she didn't tell me," Mark responded. "How did it burn Sandy and not the tree?"

"I don't know." Colin shook his head as he looked down. "Except, for the moment, she's breathing and we need to get her outta here."

No one seemed to know what to do. Cassie took a step toward the others and paused as she saw more light moving by the bottom of the slope. She had a better view than the rest of the kids as the will-o'-the-wisps started to leave the creek, and chills ran down her spine. None of her friends realized how dangerous these things were.

"Everyone duck!" she screamed.

The orbs flew. They moved with ease, edging around the nude limbs of the various hardwoods. They appeared to be accelerating, looking more like meteors about to slam into something. The sparse pines' canopies hung well above the will-o'-the-wisps' low altitudes, and now, these things shot right at the group.

Cassie struggled with believing what was in front of her. They illuminated everything around them, though no trees caught fire. These things were astounding but still made her knees shake. She knew they all needed to get away.

Zane and Mark stepped back from Sandy. Nick didn't move, and Darlene leaned over Sandy, adding a protective layer, the phone light smothered out between their bodies. Cassie couldn't catch what Colin did, but he appeared to cover up Sandy and Darlene. Now, it was too dark, and without the glow of technology, only the orbs were visible. Cassie worried for her friends, for Sandy, for what would happen next. In no way were they getting away from those things unscathed.

As the wisps moved toward the group, two grew in size. Between their speed and her being uphill looking down, Cassie had difficulty determining the diameter, but she knew they were bigger than the other spheres. As they drew closer, one made a hissing sound, and before her next breath, the two larger balls engulfed Zane and Mark. The lights began to shrink and retreated faster than they arrived.

Cassie's sight adjusted to the dark. There wasn't a bright flash of light as before. From what she'd seen, this didn't bode well for either boy swallowed by the orbs. She couldn't find them as she began to distinguish moving shapes under the moonlight. Her heart sank, and she doubted Zane or Mark were anywhere near.

Colin, Darlene, and Nick shined their phones where the other two boys once stood. All anyone saw was the wooded underbrush.

"Where'd they go?" Darlene asked.

Her question went unanswered, as Sandy bolted upright and screeched something incomprehensible. Cassie jumped, and her eyes focused on her friend.

As Sandy approached in the night, there was no way Cassie could tell exactly how much the teen was burned, though she did catch a glimpse or two. Sandy's hair on her right side no longer existed, and dark marks highlighted her face all along the right side.

Another round of will-o'-the-wisps broke from the creek bed. Their bright illumination oozed a glow across the meadow as they started moving up, breaking Cassie's concentration on her friend.

Sandy took off, running right past Cassie, with Nick and Darlene hot on her trail.

"Run, Cassie," Colin yelled.

Cassie ran, right behind Darlene and Sandy. The gravel being kicked up from the other two girls stung like little paint balls being shot right into her shins. As fast as they moved, she identified Nick as a spot along the hearse path. He sped far ahead of them. She found it odd he didn't hang back to help with Sandy.

Cassie thought Sandy's adrenaline had kicked in since she took off as though nothing had happened to her. Cassie did her best to keep up and finally caught Sandy when the injured girl stopped. Her friend's wounds were easier to identify under the moonlight. There was enough contrast to see the young teen's charred flesh mixed with glistening chunks of exposed meat. The clumps reminded Cassie of one time she had microwaved a hot dog for too long. Cassie was unsure but thought parts of Sandy's skull were visible. Her horrified thoughts rattled her inner core as the shock of what happened to her friend sank into her forethoughts. She clenched her jaws as she pictured

Sandy scarred forever from the burns and wondered if the hair would grow back along the open head wounds. Cassie needed to get her friend to the church as soon as possible.

Sandy gasped. She brought in such a considerable amount of air through a heavy hoarseness she sounded like a ragged running generator. Sandy's mouth moved as if she was trying to say something.

Cassie touched Sandy's healthy shoulder and patted it.

"Maybe you shouldn't talk," Cassie said.

"I burned," Sandy stated, a thick, hoarse sound, almost guttural, her voice strong and forced.

"I know." Cassie studied Sandy. "Jimmy already went to get an adult. They should be calling an ambulance." The pungent smell wafted around, causing her to scrunch her nose. She tried not to gag as a tear welled up. She couldn't fathom how something so awful was happening.

"They'll need more than one."

Cassie glanced behind them. More spheres gathered around the maple. Colin stood a few feet back.

"Sorry, Cass," Colin said. "Hey, if those things head this way, I'll try to slow them down."

Cassie looked at her favorite tree. The spheres circled and headed over to the hearse path.

"How?" Cassie asked.

"Never mind," he said and took off toward the lights.

"See." The harshness in Sandy's voice deepened.

"Can you move?"

"Wait."

They both watched Colin head for the now speeding spheres. The quickness in which the orbs moved still astounded Cassie, but Colin's body was getting larger. Cassie realized he was headed toward them.

"Go," he yelped.

Cassie kept Sandy's arm around her, and they ambled along the crushed gravel. A shout, a bunch of voices, and even a scream erupted as the parents ran toward them.

In a quick motion, Cassie's uncle whisked Sandy up in his arms and headed for the church. Her own legs gained speed without the weight of her friend, she bolted into her father's hug, and by the time Colin caught up to them, the nemesis had disappeared.

IT TOOK FOREVER for the ambulance to reach them. A fire truck arrived as well, and though they investigated the area around the maple and down to the creek, they found nothing. No burn marks. No trace of Zane or Mark. First responders still searched. No signs of the wisps or anything else described by Colin, Nick, Darlene, Jimmy, and Cassie.

Cassie held Sandy's good hand while Sandy's mom cried away. Cassie spoke reassuring words as calmly as she could without actually looking directly at her friend. Out of nowhere, Sandy would become alert and, with a deep, raspy voice, say, "I burned."

The paramedics rushed Sandy onto the ambulance, as well as her mother. Sandy screamed. It resonated like a constant wail without any interruption from a breath. A moment later, a paramedic approached Cassie.

"We have to keep her calm," the woman said to Cassie. "She is asking for you and wants you with her."

So Cassie climbed aboard. She did not have to ask her parents; she knew they would want her to go if that's what Sandy needed. She sat on a board next to her friend as the two paramedics kept working on the wounded teen.

"It's like there's no pulse," the paramedic said.

Sandy rolled her head to Cassie. Her good side focused on Cassie.

"I burned," Sandy said.

Cassie held Sandy's hand. "Sorry."

Sandy's one opened eye glazed over. Then a familiar scratchy alto voice came forth from a glowing orange mouth.

"And you'll burn too, Cassie."

The words were slow and precise, without any movement from Sandy's lips. Before Cassie's name was said, she was already rushing for the closed doors, shoving people and equipment aside. The crashing machine startled Sandy's mother, and the paramedic's shocked expression turned to concern as she returned her attention to Sandy.

The whole back of the ambulance heated up before Cassie reached the release handle. Her insides broiled as the high-pitched noise grew. Heat radiated up from within her own body, into her neck, and as she looked out the back door window, she saw Colin and Jimmy staring back at her. Colin should be in here, not her.

Cassie understood at that precise moment what it felt like to be cooked alive as her body baked to the point she lost the ability to move. She wanted to scream, but her abdomen wouldn't allow her to inhale. Jimmy became her focus. His head tilted like a curious dog as the heat ignited items around her. She froze as her torso felt like it was about to combust, and her eyes melted. Her last thoughts centered around getting out, but those were fleeting, as her body exploded, engulfing the ambulance in flames.

beer in a bar

· · ·

Dean savored each bite from his meal as though it were his last. He sunk the final morsel of bread into the au jus and let the taste melt in his mouth. The tanginess brought a smile to his face.

He loved food, and as a road warrior, he managed to sample some of the best cuisine around the world. For the most part, pub entrees surprised him. He didn't always desire fancy eats, those three course gems covered by a daily per diem, but he sometimes found delight in something as simple as a French dip. This particular sustenance definitely fixed his exhausted mood.

He checked his phone and regretted it. Not enough time had passed for him to stop looking for her texts. Every time he did, too many painful memories crashed his consciousness.

"You're married?" a woman asked while grabbing his ring finger, lifting his whole hand as if to obtain a closer inspection of his wedding band.

His inner thoughts dissipated. Her upbeat mood intruded on his personal space.

"Yes," he said.

"Why are you here?"

"Food and beer."

He pointed to his unfinished pint and barren plate. Her brows creased as if she didn't believe him, or she had another question.

"Is she here?"

"No."

"So empty seat?"

"Yes."

She slipped onto the red vinyl-covered stool. Her hair bounced as she settled. She waved the bartender over. With a toothy grin, she turned back to him with an extended hand.

"Anna."

"Dean."

They performed a quick shake. She turned his hand.

"Manicure?"

"Yes."

The mixologist walked up, and Anna maintained her cheerfulness while turning to order. "Gin and tonic," she said while holding out her credit card to open a tab, then turned her attention back to Dean. "Interesting."

"What?"

She gave the slightest shake of her head as if it helped her contemplate an answer. The pause allowed for the appearance of a more pensive response.

"People with money tend to be well groomed."

He chuckled. "I assure you I have to go to work every morning like everyone else."

"Sure you do."

He didn't respond and ignored her by checking out his empty plate. The way things sounded, she appeared to be having a conversation with someone else. Not only did she have a space-invading kind of happy personality but brought a lot of volume with every word. He thought she was nervous being around strangers in a bar and obviously unaware of his somber, wanting-to-be-left-alone persona. At least, he thought he gave off that particular vibe.

He reached for his almost depleted pint and took the last swallow. Before he set the empty down, the bartender pointed, and Dean nodded. One more should be okay. Besides, he did not want to sit in a hotel room all night.

No longer than a minute passed for a refreshed glass. In the meantime, he struggled not to check his phone. For years, he and his wife kept in touch through texts. A life-changing event had to occur for him to realize they maintained contact more when he was away than when they were together. Instead, he studied the worn wooden bar top. The dark stain almost gave the place a true English pub ambience, but he pondered if this was by design or luck.

"Done with the plate?" the barman asked.

"Yes."

The artwork on the man's hand stood out to Dean. A detailed eye on the back of the hand alone, with very ornate vines entwining around the wrist. He wanted to see more, but the long black sleeve of the shirt covered what he thought would have been at least a grand's worth of investment.

The bartender took off with the dinnerware before Dean could comment about the ink. Exceptional artistry fascinated him, and quite a few people wore some of the best. For his one and only, it did not turn out well. Being inebriated tended to lead him into making poor decisions, and picking out a tattoo artist named Shaky Bob became a big one. Plus, his wife hated any sort of tat, so he did not try to repurpose or cover it. After a couple of beach summers, the trembling sketch faded and lacked the same standout quality when he had first obtained the thing. Funny thing how life meandered on its own course; now, an opportunity existed for something new.

He peeked at his phone. Damn. A twinge gripped the empty pit in his chest. One he related to sorrow and depression, since he moped after such a thing happened. Dean continued to stare at the screen, lost in thought. Maybe one of his kids texted. Then again, maybe not.

The lack of any relationships with them was on him, and he owned it. He stayed on the road or worked long hours and didn't attend the usual list of events overachieving children tended to have while growing up. They were tremendous girls. He loved the family vacations, but the love of his life was who did all the parenting, thus bonding with all three of their daughters. He had no idea how to gain a relationship with them, other than to be patient and keep trying.

"You still married?" Anna asked.

"Yes," he said with rapidly successive nods.

Her eyes wavered. He ascertained she drank more than she should have in her few minutes with her friends. She possibly consumed some shots while conversing with the others around her. He concluded she probably took a little something extra.

"Well, that's too bad, but please let me know if anything changes."

She laughed and turned back to who he assumed were friends. To Dean, younger Anna offered none of the charm his wife exhibited. Plus, he actually loved his longtime bride. Though he spent most of his career away from home, he made sure they travelled together. He flew her first class on each vacation, and for every location, he'd already experienced the lay of the land. He maintained acquaintances at the right places to obtain the maximum enjoyment for their adventures. As far as he believed, she always appreciated those. He wanted everything to be special for her and did his best by her. Including never cheating. That kind of thing never interested him, and he lacked the desire now.

Someone else sat on the other side of him, taking him away from his self-reflection. He glanced at his cell again and deemed stopping such a habit as impossible. He wished way too often for her to pull off what Houdini did not and make the connection from the great beyond. He sighed, turned the device face down, and gazed at his empty glass. He chuckled and thought about how fast that one went down.

"Another?" the bartender asked.

"Yes," Dean responded, then added, "Any meaning about the eye?"

The barman stared blankly at Dean, then smiled. "Not really. My aunt is an artist, and we kind of came up with this sleeve concept together. She's awesome, and because of being family, it's the only way I could afford this."

The man unbuttoned the cuff and rolled it up to show a bit more. The vines, which ended into the eye on the back of the hand, went up the arm but wove into many patterns, such as a face, a flower, and a wolf. It was all Dean had the chance to make out before the man slid the fabric down.

"It's the full length. It took a couple of months, around five four-hour sessions."

"Amazing," Dean said. " I guess you can't get away with showing biceps here?"

"Only on manager-less days. Uniform here is black shirts, long sleeves," he said, then gave a nod toward the windows behind Dean. "That's something to make a crappy drive home."

The bartender went off to pull another pour. Dean turned to see the front door. The patio he'd passed through after coming down the stairs from the sidewalk was completely covered in a cloud. He'd experienced Seattle smothered in the murky soup before but never quite this heavy.

"Fascinating," a feminine voice stated. The word came from the non-Anna side.

"What's that?" he asked, still staring at the fog. He hoped this guest was nothing like Anna.

"The permanency of ink," she said.

He caught the slightest hint of an accent. Unsure of where from, but it reminded him of an old Romanian friend.

He faced her and became captivated by her allure. The dark hair and eyes came accentuated by a sallowness. He thought she might be ill. High cheeks, a crisp jawline, thin nose, and almost completely translucent skin. Though terribly pale, she had a familiarity about her. He focused on her in an attempt to place her.

"I'm Esther," she said.

He didn't know how to respond. The words to introduce himself did not come to mind. Almost as if she controlled his thoughts.

"Spellbound?" she asked.

Her question broke the enchantment. He caught himself.

"Oh, sorry," he said. "I'm Dean." He didn't turn away. At this moment, he was only aware of her. He tried to think of something else to say. "Can I get you a drink?"

Her eyes pierced him. "I don't think anyone is working."

He glanced around the bar, which had been manned by three people the whole time he sat there. They apparently left. The place had become packed, but there was only a fraction of the crowd, with those remaining seemingly almost sedated. He found the current emptiness odd and himself a bit ignored with no one around to take an order.

"Wow," Anna said from his other side, "check out the fog."

A number people glanced toward the door, as did Dean again. The dense vapor made the glass doors and windows appear as though they had been coated with spray paint.

"I didn't think it ever got this thick here?" he asked aloud.

"Mist forms in many ways," Esther responded.

Her reply elicited a look from his overly cheerful neighbor, who leaned across him.

"He's married," Anna said.

"Monogamous?" Esther questioned.

Anna shrugged, and he nodded.

"How castigating," Esther added.

"If he decides not to be married, I had him first," Anna stated right to Esther.

The pallid woman didn't change her facial demeanor. Dean's wide-eyed expression appeared to be missed by the young woman, who sat back with her own jovial face, then turned her conversation to her friends.

"Possessive," Esther commented as she stared at him.

"I've agreed to nothing of the sort," he said, and her smile never faltered. "Besides, I have kids older than her. I think."

"Sounds like an occasion for aberration," she said, reaching over and patting his arm. "I believe you."

Her steady expression unnerved him. In the back of his mind, danger existed behind her reassurance. He didn't fathom how, and the thought evaporated the more he concentrated on her.

Her hand slid onto the bar near his. The comparison of his color next to hers made her own skin unnatural in every way. It was as if someone washed away her pigmentation.

"I'm unusually pale," Esther said as she examined her own hand pressed against the side of his.

He noted not only her pallidness but also how long her fingernails extended. They were almost sharp to a point and, due to the thickness, made him think of claws.

With a sudden urge to confess, Dean leaned closer to Esther. "Actually, my wife passed … four months ago." He paused and took a breath. "So yes, technically, I am not married, but I still act as such."

"Hmm, still act as such?" He took her question as rhetorical. "And now she's dead?" He had no doubt he could lose himself in her eyes. They were dark to the point her irises were opaque. There was only a subtle color difference with the pupil. Yet the small smirk had a definite shit-eating quality to it. "Not till death do us part?"

Dean was unsure on how to respond. He wished he had never blurted out his true status. His stomach acid started tracking up through his esophagus, the subtle burning rising inside. "Not for me."

"Hmm." She nodded. "Not for me." Her eyes focused on his. "You miss her?"

"Every minute of every day."

"What do you miss about her?"

"Every part of her, from her beauty to her wonderful wit." He paused through a deep breath. "She was way smarter than me."

"Hmm, smarter. This is what you miss?"

"Actually, yes." He glanced at his beer and peered around for bartenders. "One of many things about her that I miss. Well, not the thing she did that was as obnoxious as an ad in a movie. She'd always give three possible explanations and start with saying, 'would you believe.' Something she picked up from an old TV show."

"You miss such obnoxiousness now?"

"I do, though at the time, her little routine caused me to become completely unhinged." He wiped his eyes a bit. A tear did not form, but water built on his bottom eyelashes. "She was an amazing person, and I miss her."

"Was she a doctor or a scientist? Or a professor?"

"No." He thought it sort of funny Esther asked. "She wanted to go to med school and even got accepted to several close to home, but in the end, she decided not to go."

"Hmm, she decided." Esther peered back to the kitchen. "I wonder why she would go through the trouble only to decide against going."

"Economics. She was almost fifty; by the time she'd finish any residency, she'd be near sixty. There's simply no way to get a return on the investment."

"Hmm, return on investment." She nodded. "So brain power, this is why you don't like *her*," Esther said, pointing at Anna.

"It's not a matter of like." He creased his brows and glanced the younger woman's direction. "I'm just not interested."

"Hmm, not interested."

A new mixologist walked up. Her short hair emphasized a long neck with sharp facial features. She wore a sleeveless black leather blouse. It lacked shape, nor did it accentuate any body parts but fit blocky, almost like scrubs. With one hand, decorated with the identical style of fingernails as the woman sitting next to him, she placed a filled wine glass in front of Esther.

"A recent vintage," she said.

Esther lifted the drink by the stem. She held it up to the ceiling lights and then swirled the liquid. After, she brought it under her nose. Dean heard her inhale. He regarded, with interest, as Esther showed considerable patience in her tasting, as well as pure gratification. She sampled the dark, crimson contents, and he thought of the last bite of his own meal and how he'd savored the moment. She must have been doing the same.

Her eyes closed. The small grin she'd maintained for as long as she'd sat next to him finally widened. Dean thought he saw a tinge of rouge appear on her cheeks.

"That good?" he asked.

"You have no idea," Esther said while opening her eyes, focusing on him. She took another sip.

"Would you like some?" the new mixologist asked Dean.

"Oh, no, thank you, I tend not to mix when drinking." He pointed at his beer.

The bartender left while he studied Esther relishing her drink. He wished he appreciated anything as much as she did this. The whole display of her partaking and her enjoyment brought out a glamor he had to have missed before. She was gorgeous in an exotic way, but this was like viewing a supermodel perform in front of a camera. He became aware of his own fixation on her and chastised himself for staring so intently at her.

"Am I making a show?"

Her question intruded on his observation. Obviously, he had been caught doing more than watching.

"I haven't quite seen anyone be this grateful for wine."

"Hmm, grateful indeed."

He chuckled. "Indeed."

Her dark eyes consumed him. The thought of holding her flashed across his mind. With tremendous effort, he stared at his beer and not her. It had only been four months. He shouldn't think like that. He may not have been the most attentive husband in the world, but he still loved his wife. His heart ached, damnit.

Something within her long almond eyes. They were so dark and soothing. He had a deep desire to disappear in them. His faint inner voice told him bad things surrounded him, he needed to observe anything other than her face. He fixated on her bare arms. Somehow, her skin was less translucent than before. Possibly her drink restored her like his meal had done for him. Except he wasn't ever deathly pallid.

She nudged him, bringing his gaze back to her face as she raised her eyebrows as if to question him.

"Oh, nothing." He shifted in his chair, then used his finger to circle the air around his face. "It appears the wine refreshed you a bit." He simpered in an attempt to feign happiness to cover his nervousness, and his focus was drawn into the bottomless pools of her eyes. Yes, he wanted to be enamored by her and to never glance away again.

He liked the confidence behind her relaxed expression, and the way she held her chin gave her more of a regal bearing. From way back in the crevice of his mind, the earlier thought of danger yelled at him, but he lacked the understanding as to why. He sure as shit didn't need another beer, but he needed a reason to continue to sit next to her. He thought about ordering a water.

She nodded. Her countenance remained relaxed yet commanding. She stared into him as if grabbing hold of his soul. The draw to her came from deep within. All he wanted was to dive back into her and grasp any part of her, never to let go. This wasn't physical but emotional, as if his heart already belonged to her. Nothing about what he desired was sexual—he yearned for something more.

He blinked a few times as if coming out of a stupor.

"My thoughts," he said. "I may have had a beer too many, since my mind seems to be cloudy."

"Must have come with the murk outside."

"Yeah."

"Would you like to have a stroll?"

"Yeah, stroll." He nodded, riveted on her.

Esther began to get up, as did he.

The leather clad bartender came up as if waiting for an instruction.

"Rochelle," Esther said, "his is my charge."

"As you wish," Rochelle responded.

"When did you get her name?" Dean asked.

"I frequent here"

"Reg-u-lar." His speech was slow, with a solid effort on all three syllables. He chuckled. *Wow*, he thought, *and only after a few beers*. Somewhere along the way, he had become a real lightweight.

"Sir," Rochelle said, "don't forget your phone."

He blindly picked up the device, his mind heavy as if in a dream.

Anna pushed through between Dean and the bar. "Hey," she said, pointing at Dean. Her legs faltered once she faced Esther. "Where are you guys going?"

"We are retiring for the evening," Esther answered.

Anna dropped her hand and abruptly raised her finger again, directed right back at Dean. "But he's married."

"And what does piernik have to do with a windmill?"

Dean didn't quite understand all the words but caught on to her probably comparing one unrelated thing to another. He stared at Anna, waiting for her to respond.

She wavered a bit in her stance as she attempted to say something.

"What?" Her question came out almost as unsteady as she appeared.

He missed Rochelle moving from behind the bar but saw her walk up behind Anna, placing her arm around the woman's shoulders.

"Are you okay?" Rochelle asked her.

Anna motioned to nod, but as she glanced up at Rochelle, she changed her reply to no.

"I'll take her," another server in a white short-sleeved blouse said. This one was pale as well but nowhere near as colorless as Esther. Dean ascertained there was another employee out of the bar's uniform. She escorted Anna in the direction of the restrooms.

"When do you start your next shift?" Esther asked Rochelle.

"A few minutes ago, but I need to clean up here."

"In this weather, it's safer to walk with us." Esther nodded toward the bar. "Ask Amara if she approves."

Rochelle went to another bartender. Dean tried to say something, but the words never surfaced. He thought if he didn't watch all the commotion around him, he might be able to focus. He forced his head down in order to stare at his shoes. His frontal lobe berated him for not staring into Esther's eyes. After a couple of seconds of being attentive to his feet, the self-chastising stopped, and it became easier to keep his head downward.

But the urge to study Esther still remained. He missed her. He searched for something else. The memory of his wife. Something safe. Something real. The familiar pang in his chest rang true but, somehow, was not as strong as the impulse to admire Esther. Those dark pools of timeless curiosity. He desired to be there. They were peaceful. Here in his mind with his eyes cast down, he yearned for the woman he'd just met.

"Where is her next shift?" he asked without ever looking up.

"At the hotel where I reside." Esther's voice lured him to face her. How he loved to gaze at her. "Dean, shall we?" He nodded. "No one should ever walk in this gloom alone," she added.

"Yeah, alone." His eyes never left her.

She went beyond her smug expression to show the whiteness of her teeth. "Thank you for the escort."

He gave a simple nod as if he was a formally trained gentlemen and held out the crook of his arm. She slid her arm around his at the elbow as they headed toward the doors. Rochelle followed. Dean glanced once more around the restaurant. The amount of patrons had decreased, and barely a murmur carried throughout the floor. The particular thing that bothered him was none of the servers wore black long-sleeve shirts. The manager had to be out, and Dean pondered if this was the only change.

Navigating the outdoor patio proved to be a challenge for him due to the impossibility of seeing the tables even as they stood next to one. No customers sat outdoors. The classic '80s rock playing inside was louder outside. He turned back to the glass doors they'd exited, only a few feet behind him, but did not see them. The fog encompassed everything around their group, and for some reason, his initial worry about going forward dissipated. He found a sense of security within the dense air blanket.

Dean kept steady and allowed Esther to lead the way. Obviously, Esther frequented the pub many times before, as she navigated the patio so well. He lacked the awareness of the stairs but took each step when Esther did. Before he realized it, they were on street level.

The music became distant as they walked away from the restaurant. They took a left on the pavement.

"Where are we headed?" he asked.

"To the Mayflower," Esther said.

"Yes, the Mayflower," he said as another arm wrapped around his elbow on his free side. "I reside there." Dean smirked in an attempt to please Esther instead of showing his sheer joy of basking in her presence. He was aware of Rochelle, who now clung to his other side, but in no way did he want to break away from his view of Esther.

It was not long before they reached the intersection. Dean was unsure since the traffic lights hid underneath the dense urban nebula, but the echo of street lamps in the fog created enough glare for him to see as he moved along the sidewalk where they crossed the road. They turned left, journeying along Pike.

He did pry his attention away from Esther to check ahead a few times, but each time, his head drifted back to where he could peek at her. Though she never glanced his way, her profile inveigled him. He only wanted her.

They turned right, and Dean recalled the hotel wasn't far. He remembered there should be a park, but they wouldn't be able to see it in the opaque vapor anyway. On his way for a meal earlier, he'd wondered how the area would seem at night. It was a small city plaza but appeared to be a great place to hang out. Well, not for his age bracket, but there had been plenty of younger people there all day. Some with longboards, others talking in groups. They were there when he went to work and still there when he returned in the late afternoon. Except an hour later, just before dark, when he left to find something to eat, all those kids and youths had simply vanished with no signs the park had been occupied by them earlier in the day.

Now, his observations did not matter, only Esther did. He'd never met anyone as enticing as her. That he had not checked his phone popped in his mind, and for a second, a flash of an internal debate began about if the mourning for his wife was over. Even if it had been only four months. The familiar pang erupted once again but faded.

Though he walked between their grasps, he really followed. What would happen next? Dean did not know. He hoped to only be their escort back to the hotel, but he realized he was being led. More like pulled. With the faint warnings in his head in the distance, he no longer had the urge to resist. He went. On top of it all, once he'd pushed back those deep thoughts, he found contentment.

Seeing the buildings snapped him into the moment. He missed the park in the fog, and the mist seemed to have lightened up, since he could see various entrances, all with *Closed* signs, as they passed.

On entering the hotel, the cloud dissipated. Inside, no one else occupied the lobby. They came through the side doors close to the elevator bank. Everything, though old fashioned, appeared clean and well kept, including the lift buttons and door. Dean took a glimpse of the empty front desk; it was only the three of them.

He turned to Rochelle, who had no expression on her face of any sort. Her stare reflected back to him as blank as he felt. He switched back to Esther. She maintained her slight smile, that continuous coprophagous grin. It was possible he'd had too much to drink.

In no time, they were opening the door to Esther's room. When they entered the space, he realized it was bigger than any other room he had ever stayed in at the hotel. He had no idea the old building packed a room this size. They must be on one of the higher floors. Come to think of it, he never did ask what Esther did for a living, nor did she ask him.

The ornate curtains and extra tapestry around the window were the same in his room, but he didn't have a table with chairs, or love seats, or a coffee table and sofa. This was a definite suite. It rocked all the hotel neutral colors but held its own level of individuality, which seemed to fit this place and nowhere else.

She came close to him. He didn't hear her breathing or feel it, but she was near enough he should have sensed it. Her lips almost touched his. He wanted them to touch, but then again, he didn't. He stood there with his eyes closed. The pang in his chest became larger. He could not do this. He was not ready.

"Still married?" Esther asked.

He silently indicated yes. So this was why he conjured up the unusually foul halitosis. It reminded him of the dead rat he had to pull out from underneath his shed. Her stench was undeniably the identical smell. Rotted animal flesh. Death. Decay. This lingered from inside her mouth.

What he sensed was impossible. She'd had only wine at the bar and nothing to eat. So the scent came from his head, something subconsciously made up to throw him off from liking her, and he thanked his internal self.

She backed away from him, raised her eyebrows up, and, with a playful grin, asked, "Did I offend?"

He shook his head, and though he desired those mystifying eyes, he closed his own to keep from them. The eagerness to stare at her faded moment by moment.

"Why don't you relax on the sofa?" she said.

Rochelle took him by the arm as an escort. He was thankful he was able to sit without seeing where to put his backside. He imagined Esther spied his every move. It must have been Rochelle who sat next him. Well, almost on him. Her leg squeezed right next to his, and her hand landed on his lap. He wanted to brush it away but thought it was best not to interfere. He wasn't sure what they were after, but it was apparent they desired something.

Dean heard some movement, followed by the slight scuff of something being lifted from the floor, then moved to be in front of him. Most likely a chair. Then he knew when someone settled on it. He assumed it was Esther.

"Let's learn the chalk from the cheese," Esther said.

"Let's not," he responded. "Just let me go back to my room."

"Can't do that now. You realize that."

"No, I only had a tad too much to drink." He hoped this worked.

"Two things you should know." She paused with a sigh. "One is I hate lies. Lying to me is—" She hesitated. "What's today's slang for it? ...Yes, about as useful as nuts on a priest, because I know, without a doubt, when a lie is presented. Just as I know what you said is a non-truth."

Dean didn't know what to say, much less what to do. He only wanted to go back to his room and sleep this off. He maintained pleasantries to her all evening and even walked her back to the hotel. Why couldn't she just leave him alone?

"By the way," her words were smooth, controlling, and comforting, "your closed eyes doesn't work. I'm already in your head."

He still wasn't going to open his eyes or move Rochelle's hand. It lay still. She wasn't moving it or caressing him, so it was only an extra weight. He thought it was kind of nice, and he knew exactly where she was, and by sound, he had an idea where Esther sat.

"For example, I can flash an image in your head. One that will cause an instant reaction."

More than a picture flashed across his mind. A movie took over his brain. Something like a hologram he could not shut off or turn away from. One of Esther and Rochelle standing in front of him, clad in lingerie, and making out. The smacks of the lips caressed his nerves; a citrus scent filled his nostrils, followed by lavender. The last odor was one his wife burned from a candle whenever he returned home from trips. He felt his arousal.

"That was fast," Rochelle said, moving her hand.

He ignored the comment and thought he heard movement. Possibly others entered the suite or were there already.

"Now, open your eyes," Esther commanded.

He did as instructed. Esther stood in front of him and behind a chair, where another woman sat. He recognized her immediately, but what he saw was impossible. He blinked a few times.

"Barbara?" he asked.

"Hi, dear," the woman said. "Is that for me, or Rochelle, or Esther?" She pointed at his crotch.

"What have you done to me," he said. "This isn't funny."

"Oh, I concur, it's not humorous, especially to make an agreement, then to not honor it." Esther nodded in the direction of the woman who sat in front of her and resembled his deceased wife.

"What did I not honor?"

Rochelle leaned into him and whispered in his ear: "Med school."

"I didn't say not to go." He stared at the woman he still didn't believe was his wife.

"Correct, you didn't, but you did make it seem like if I went, then it would have been the most selfish and stupid thing I could ever had done," Barbara said. Except this phrase did sound like her. He didn't know how they pulled this off, but she was an exact duplicate of his bride, as was her voice and her sayings, her mannerisms. But the type of clothes she wore at the moment was not her style.

"I saw you dead. I was there when the doctor said."

"Well, would you believe in walking miracles? Or better yet, I didn't like the other side." She giggled. "Or how about I'm just a plain ol' creature of the night."

"Bullshit. I don't know how you're doing this."

She slapped her hands down on her legs, appearing to be a bit frustrated. "You went against my last wishes for me to be buried and signed me right up for cremation."

"When did you say you wanted to be buried?"

"Anytime we talked about it." She placed her hands on her hips. "Thanks for listening. Plus, you ignored the file in the safe where I had bought the plots for us both along with the tombstone. Luckily, Esther intercepted my body; otherwise, I'd been really pissed to wake up in hell."

She took the chair and scooted it against him. The edge pressed against his knees, and his feet were under the seat. Barbara sat right in front of him and spread her legs to where his knees were on the inside of hers. Her short dress revealed her thighs, and Dean glanced at where a mole on the inside of each leg matched the other. She lifted her skirt up and stretched out.

"Is this what you are looking for?" she asked, pointing at the beauty marks.

They were the same and in the exact spot he caressed many times through their marital intimacies. He stared into her eyes. The irises were the same color of amber they had always been. This was impossible. She was dead.

"I don't know how you are doing this …"

"Dean, honey, look at me." She smiled a big, toothy smile, exposing sharp canines.

"This doesn't scare me. I know fake teeth when I see them." He paused, thinking of an additional response. Nothing came to mind. "What do you want? Who are you?"

Esther's grin widened. "I think you know what we are." This time, she expanded her lips.

Dean glanced over at Rochelle, who showed her teeth as well. Her canines were as pointed as the others. He sighed. "Stop messing around."

Esther never wavered. "It's amazing how humanity can ignore the supernatural even when standing right in front them." She shook her head as if she disapproved of him. Then her smile disappeared. "And it really pisses me off." Her words were cold. Her once charming eyes steeled and now penetrated right through him. The anger shot into him, causing his hardened condition to dissipate.

Dean sat up as much as he could. It was an attempt to defy her, all of them. He made sure his back was straight and his shoulders squared. He stared at Esther. If he was going to be killed, he might as well face it all head-on.

Esther resumed a relaxed position, and her smirk returned, as she no longer focused on Dean. "Thank you for coming tonight," Esther said to a group of women he suddenly became aware of as they stood on either side of Esther, all in front of him. Many he recognized from the restaurant.

He knew they vilified him and felt like rabbit displayed in a wolves' den. The realization from the experience with his recent condition, through the fog, the bar, the walk home, and how quickly he became fascinated with Esther, his racing thoughts of vampires and his dead wife—it was possible this could be real.

He started to shake, tears flowed, and he took shallow gasps of air. He glanced up at Barbara. "This can't be you. You'd never be mean or hurt anyone."

"Let's just say, betrayal changes one's nature."

"I never betrayed you. I've never been with another woman."

"I know. I'm still talking about med school. When we married, we shared our dreams together. Mine was to have kids first, then go on to become a doctor. I even received a master's to get prepped to go. I was accepted to every med school I applied to, and you said to wait until our youngest was in high school. Remember?"

"You agreed."

"Yes, only until our last daughter reached high school, but did I have a choice?"

For some reason, he peered over at Rochelle, her blank look with the same slight smile she kept on her face, same as all the others. He was the only one on his side, no matter how cozied up to him she happened to be at the moment.

"And then our youngest started high school," she said, "and I got accepted again to every school in the area. And you said it didn't make financial sense to pursue such a thing. I was shattered."

Dean could see the furrowed brows and scathing, squinted eyes. He recognized her chagrin. She never held her anger in check, but not once did she display the clenched fists she held at her side by straight arms. Then she raised her hand and pointed right at him.

"I should rip your throat out, just on principle."

He shook his head. "This isn't you. I was good to you. I gave you everything."

"Except what I wanted and you agreed to do when we first started out."

"That's not true. You agreed with me."

"No." Her voice softened. "I never did. However, I did agree with Esther."

Dean considered the woman he first met earlier in the evening. He could not believe he'd even thought about being with her. He hated her and blamed her for everything.

"Blame yourself," Esther said. "Besides, it's a small matter. We all are born crying, live complaining, and die disappointed."

Dean sobbed and lost himself, blubbering away. No way this was all his fault. Barbara had agreed with the decision when she was a supportive wife. Somehow, he'd received a death sentence with her becoming undead.

Esther stepped toward him, reached down, and patted his knee. "Compose yourself, dragul meu."

"Listen," Barbara said, "I thought for sure you were not only redoing the definitions of our marriage but also cheating on me. For that, I was going to tear your heart out, but because you're only a selfish ass, I'm going easy on you." She laughed, stood, and walked away.

"What now?" he asked, viewing his former wife's back.

"Rochelle knows what to do," she said without turning around.

Within a few seconds, everyone in the room vanished and the lights dimmed. He was unsure if they disappeared into thin air or if they walked out of the room. Everything moved too fast for him. Rochelle moved and extended her hand to him. She escorted him out of the suite and to the elevator. They took the ride down to his floor, to his room, where he opened the door, and Rochelle led the way inside.

"What now?" he asked again.

"I'll carry out the sentence."

"But I don't want to die. I didn't do anything wrong."

"You killed a dream. You were, at the least, a party to it dying. So yes, you did something wrong."

A tear formed and trickled down his cheek. Rochelle kissed the wetness and smiled at him. His tears stopped.

"It's way too late for tears," she said. "Don't worry, you'll die like a man. I know how important that is to you fellows."

She took him over to the bed, where she turned to kiss him, and they both sat.

"Why are you being nice to me?"

"Because, well, you remind me of my old boyfriend."

"What happened to him?"

"He was killed in the Battle of the Bulge." She sighed. "I met Esther one night after I found out he'd died. She said if I joined her, we could put an end to the war. So I did, and we went." Her eyes searched around the room. "It's an arduous and burdensome task for us to travel, especially over bodies of water, but we went, taking our coffins full of our native soil, finding great places to operate from, and proceeded to create a ton of havoc."

Dean repositioned himself with his back on two pillows, leaning against the headboard. "Sounds like you are the good guys, but you just killed those people in the bar, and even poor Anna."

Rochelle laughed aloud. "No, we didn't. We take a bit of blood while implanting memories of them having sex with one another. A real superb recollection of their sexual encounter based on their own fantasies." She paused for a second. "They awake nude or partially clothed, and these thoughts flood in very much like when waking up with a hangover from a night of quaffing too many pints. Things trickle in, and people feel ashamed as they recollect. Most people are so embarrassed by how much they enjoyed it. They get dressed and go home feeling a bit weak."

"Why sexual encounters?"

"Because, still to this day, people will not talk about sex, especially their wildest fantasies. So we get our dinner without creating a trail of bodies, and the general population gets their jollies without the slightest transference of an STD. We hit different areas of the world and keep on the move."

Dean struggled with how the implanted remembrances worked.

"For example," Rochelle said and then leaned into him, giving him a long kiss where their tongues danced as his body became alive. They made out for what seemed forever, and they shed their clothes, eventually leading to making love.

Finally, Dean believed he'd regained some control over himself. His release was more intense than anything experienced before.

She rolled out of bed and stared at him as she dressed. Dean liked her green eyes and how the auburn color of her hair seemed like a natural accent. She made love with more passion than he thought was possible. His wife had not been his first lover when they married, but until now, she had been his last. Rochelle made him wish for a tomorrow.

"Tomorrow will never come for you, my dear," she said.

He sat in the bed, already dressed, as was she, standing right in front of him.

"See?" she said. "No exchange of bodily fluids. Walk me to the door?"

He accompanied her to the door. She peered into the bathroom as they went by and paused in the small foyer.

"It might be better if you moved the desk chair to right here," she said.

"Okay."

She went to open the door, and he could not help but to think of the cameras out in the hall. How they would pick her up leaving, and how they saw him come into the hotel with Esther and herself. She turned back to him as she opened the door.

"The cameras have been off all night until we stepped foot on this floor. Funny thing is I don't reflect in a mirror or show up on a recording of any type."

He wanted to seize her and live the false memory, but he appreciated it was never going to happen. She left down the hall. He stuck his head out to watch her depart. She glanced back at him.

"You're okay with just killing me," he said.

"Yes," she said. "Don't fear the next step and enjoy your shave. Be sure to nick both sides." She disappeared right before his eyes, as the others had in the suite before he returned to his room.

He closed his door and went to the desk, grabbing the chair. He placed it where Rochelle suggested, and he went into the washroom, where he turned on the shower. As the room heated up, the top of the mirror misted. He brushed his teeth and kept the sink water warm as it ran.

Dean lathered up his hands with shaving cream and applied it to his cheeks and neck. He rinsed off the razor and began his shave along his neck in strips. With each stroke, the lather disappeared, showing his smooth skin. On his fourth pass, he dug in a little farther and snagged his skin. It didn't cut deep enough, so he took an extra blade from his bag. He viewed his reflection as he sliced where his razor previously marked the spot.

He struck the correct spot. The first spurt of blood hit the mirror. He cut the other side of his neck with the blade.

His pulse increased at the sight. He calmly placed his hand over the wound without clamping down to stop the bleeding. He stepped out of the bathroom and sat on the chair he'd recently placed outside the door, where he dreamed of another moment with Rochelle and sat until he collapsed. The blood didn't clot but pumped out of him with each heartbeat, pooling around the chair.

the madhouse

. . .

Drew nodded with a broad grin. "Yes, I did."

Levi had known Drew ever since they teamed up to perform practical jokes on their first grade teacher, Ms. Cerwinski. Small things like disintegrating chalk and her desk falling apart. They drove the poor woman nuttier than a port-a-potty at a peanut festival.

Their favorite prank centered on her disappearing lunch. Somehow, it always found its way to Mr. Malone's room. Levi and Drew never dreamed their almost daily trick would play a part in her becoming Mrs. Malone. After they realized the fruit of their actions, they thought of themselves as ingenious, even though they'd brought the woman to tears more than once.

Now in their mid-fifties and after all the talks of faded dreams, Levi stood inside a former old barn to bask in the ambience of a former beer fantasy. Drew had transformed the aged structure into a Texas pub.

"Bar's open. What'll you have?" Drew asked.

"Beer me."

Drew laughed and pointed to sixteen tap handles.

"Which one?" Drew asked.

"Oh man, you overdid it."

"Yeah, don't get too excited. Only the ones on the left are active."

Levi studied the colorful pulls on the far side. "Modelo it is."

Like children hiding from the victim of their antics, they both snickered as Drew began to pour. Levi's excitement at the possibility of unlimited brew nearly caused him to reach an irrational high of giddiness. He gathered his wits and focused on the sign above the bar, designed with a murder of crows.

"The Madhouse on Madison," Levi read aloud. "Isn't that the old arena nickname for the Blackhawks?"

"Of course, and since I live out here on Madison ..."

"Damn, you realize you're the only hockey fan in Galveston County."

"Nah, there's more of us than you think, bud."

"Fake news."

"Listen, Levi," Drew said, voice lowered, brows down, and a quick look around as if to verify they were alone, "I've got something to tell you before—"

Levi heard footfalls behind him.

Drew's concerned expression evaporated into a smile. Looking toward the entrance, Drew asked, "Hannah, what'll you have?"

Levi's short hairs came to attention. His widened eyes centered on Drew. *Is she here? No way, this has to be a joke.*

"Nothing for me. I'm here for the freaky shit."

Hearing Hannah, Levi's pulse thrummed like hummingbird wings in flight. He swiveled on his stool, nearly falling off, as she approached him. His face flared hot enough to melt skin from his skull. In his gut, he had no doubt she was well aware of his discomfort. He wished the ground would open to swallow him whole.

His thoughts raced for a polished line from any book or movie he could recall, but for all the words crammed into his brain, none made his mouth move.

"Hannah?" The one-named question was uttered in more of a pubescent squeak. The last time he set eyes on her, he embarrassed himself by saying something stupid. He'd tried to pull some smooth imagery of birds and flowers together but only managed to mention something incoherent about a canary. And though it had been more than a decade since, nothing had changed.

"Hi, Levi." Her sultry sound grabbed hold of his ears and didn't let go. "You okay?"

Her unanswered inquiry hung in the air for a few awkward seconds while the gears in his head ground away. "Uh, yeah." His mind raced faster than his pulse yet delivered nothing. He needed something to say to keep her talking to him. "I thought you were gone." No one had said anything around town about her returning to their home town, but his consciousness berated himself for such a lame response. *Geesh, at least act like an adult.* He wanted to run away and cry.

"I recently returned."

Levi's jaw dropped. Imagining a conversation with her came easy for him. Being engaged in an actual sentence-to-sentence chat with her was about as relatable as having a life on Mars. Conversing with Hannah was more of a dream than reality. Much less her standing in front of him at Drew's Madhouse. To him, their little fishing village didn't fit her. She held the allure of a Manhattan penthouse socialite. A vogue he adored. Hannah should be on television or in politics and nowhere near Shoal Point.

Every day in high school, he'd wondered what it would be like to be near her, to be in the same car with her, to be out grabbing a milkshake, or sitting next to her at a movie. He learned early on none of that was meant for him.

His life's dream was to have a relationship with her, to share a life with her. Though he dated a few women over his adult life, he only wanted Hannah. If she was unavailable, he would rather be single. He hoped one day they would sit and talk the day or night away as they listened to music or read together. However, it took two sets of dreams for something like that to happen, and in no way did her future fantasies include him. Besides, they were both over fifty and with not many years left. Still, he would do anything to make that fantasy a reality.

He stared as she glided behind the bar and opened the glass door refrigerator, grabbing a bottle of Topo, amazed by her youthful appearance. She had not aged a single year, week, or day since her teenage years. He bet her high school wardrobe still fit her. Levi glanced at his beer belly; a sizable waist filled his vision. *Well, that's not good or fair.* He focused on her again. *Yep, she hasn't aged a day.*

"You can put your tongue back in your mouth, Levi," Hannah said.

"Sorry," he said, ready to self-combust, and ducked as if he were a young schoolboy getting caught admiring his teacher.

Drew placed two oversized pint glasses on the bar, sliding one closer to Levi. Trying to gather himself, Levi peeked at the amber contents bubbling up.

Drew smiled and mouthed "relax" while lifting his glass. The other two raised their drinks.

"Welcome to the Madhouse!" Drew said. The three clinked their containers.

"Cheers!" They all sipped to their toast.

"The cooler still full?" Hannah asked, downing a large portion of her bottle.

Drew set his beer on the bar and leaned close to her. "I'm guessing so." He allowed a nod toward the hallway behind them. "He said to leave it closed until he got here."

Levi worked on ignoring Hannah licking her plump lips along with the undulation of her throat as she swallowed part of her beverage, but he failed. Upon eye contact, she winked at him. *Busted.* His face blossomed once again. He changed his line of sight, scrambling for some way to take any attention off of him.

"So, what's the freaky shit?" Levi asked Drew. "What's in the back?"

"Well, remember I had something to tell you?"

His immediate conclusion was somehow Hannah and Drew became a couple. His envy for Drew achieving a dream of a bar existed but as more of a minor admiration for his best bud. Being kept out of the construction and remodeling of such an old structure left Levi butthurt. However, if Drew and Hannah were an item, then consider World War Three in full swing. Drew absorbed all of Levi's thoughts regarding Hannah over the years. They'd had many conversations about her. Levi's sudden rage rolled into his chest, where it boiled. This betrayal was almost too much.

"I thought you meant something about the bar," he said, trying to hide the anger. "I had no idea you were going out with Hannah."

Both Drew and Hannah bellowed with laughter. Once again, he reddened with embarrassment. Hannah patted Levi on the arm as she brushed past him. She sashayed to the other side of the converted barn. He continued his vigil of her as she picked up a handful of darts. With his skin still tingling from her touch, he forced his head toward Drew. He worked on his presumptions regarding Drew and Hannah .

"Dude, spill."

"You know how this place was left to me?"

"From your grandfather who'd been in the nuthouse for the last half of his life." Levi smirked and sighed. "Yeah, I wish I had a rich relative."

"I finally did some research on the land. The house was built on the bayou in the 1880s, and this barn was added sometime later. Records indicate an above-average number of murders for the population in this one-mile radius. The bizarre thing is they would find an arm laying around but never any bodies."

Memories rose in Levi's mind. "My grandparents told stories about this area, but my dad laughed about them. Does this have anything to do with your grandfather being bat shit crazy?"

"No! Nothin' to do with that. Plus, there's nothin' wrong with the land. It's dirt and grass. A serial killer probably lived nearby, and now he's long dead. It's safe." Drew's arms motioned an umpire's signal for a slide into home plate. "So, I decided to do something else with my life and do it here. Plus, I wanted a bit more on the weekends instead of hangin' at Bettie's Saloon."

Levi reflected on the past couple months, how his buddy always offered excuses for not going out. Bettie's lacked the same draw without him, but Shoal Point's working-class residents' only affordable vice after a long day's labor revolved around cheap beer and whiskey.

"Damn, Drew. I'd have helped."

"I get it, and you can with the house. If you're up for it, maybe you can have more to do with the bar." Drew paused. "For once, I wanted to build something myself. To prove I was worth more than my father thought."

"And Hannah showed up to help?" Levi asked and peeked back at her.

She jerked as if she belched and muttered something. "That's right; I did," Hannah continued to throw darts.

Did she just burp?

Levi leaned over. "Drew, did she …?" he whispered.

"Probably, she loves carbonated water. Sneaks up on her."

Levi peeked at Hannah and could not believe she hung out here. The fact she was actually in an old barn with two geeks from her old high school was impossible to fathom. Drew's words surfaced into his thoughts. He caught himself watching her and searched for something else to view. His sight landed on a pinball machine with familiar character faces.

"Addam's Family, seriously?" Levi asked.

Drew laughed. "That's the one."

"Good times." Levi's heart grew a little heavy as he became concerned. "Drew, I have so many questions. Such as, why didn't you tell me you were workin' on the barn? Why now? What do you mean *more* on the bar? Freaky shit? And how in the hell does Hannah figure into this place?"

"Funny you should mention Hannah. When I first came out here, I ran into a priest. In fact, he'll be here soon. He mentioned something about research, and she's assistin' him."

"Hannah's religious?"

"Oh, god, no," Hannah shouted as she counted her score.

Levi turned back to his long-time crush. Between Drew and her, this was more of a tennis match, watching the ball go back and forth.

"Why don't you come over here and participate in the conversation instead of yelling from across the room?" Levi asked.

"Because I can hear you mutter just fine from over here."

He found himself fixated on her again. Levi adjusted in a different direction, where he recognized a bubble hockey game. It reminded him of the one he and Drew played all night at an amusement park. They scored a bag of tokens and spent hours on it.

Levi returned to Drew. "So, no you and Hannah?"

"No." With a scowl, Drew leaned over the bar toward him. "I can't believe you'd even think that," he whispered.

Relief flooded him. *But what was she doing helping a priest, and researching what?*

All the modern legends from Shoal Point entered his mind—from the occasional and random burst of lights over the Memorial Baptist Cemetery to Wagner's old murder house on County Road 101, plus all the wild tales in between.

A shiver ran down his back. Hannah's words about the cooler, freaky shit, and Drew mentioning research took hold. The understanding struck hard.

"Drew, I've spent a lifetime avoiding all the bizarre crap this town throws at us."

"This is different."

"It ends the same."

Every cell in his body screamed at him to leave. His skin pores oozed warnings to all areas of his heart, mind, or soul that listened. Deep in his chest, a pit developed, sinking low inside him. Through the years, he gathered all the stories, and in quite a few of the cases, knew the victims and survivors. He wanted no part of any local lore. His contentment for welding came from the happiness of his customers with his work. Plus, he started a new possible side business of silversmithing jewelry, something he failed to tell anyone about, including Drew. He made the small treasures for one overseas client. He enjoyed both of those things and desired nothing more than to live a simple drinking life.

"Sunset arrives exactly three minutes earlier than forecasted," a deep voice boomed from the open doors of the barn. "We need to close up shop."

A hipster in skinny jeans entered and appeared ready for adventure as he carried two duffle bags, one in each hand.

Is this the guy? From the word *priest*, Levi pictured someone mostly gray, older kind of gentleman, not a dude wearing tattered cowboy boots and aviator sunglasses.

From the man's broad shoulders, chiseled face, and a professional athlete's physique, Levi's jealousy and sarcasm part of his brain rustled up to the top. *Sure Hannah helped with research.* Plus, he could not quite place the accent. Besides, from where Levi sat, this man exuded more playboy bravado than spiritual wisdom.

As the fellow removed his shades, Levi grasped the determined resolve behind his steel-blue eyes. The man was the epitome of confidence. When he reached the bar, he set his bags down.

"Is this your friend Levi?" the priest asked Drew, who indicated an affirmative with his thumb. "Levi, I'm Father Paul."

The two men shook hands as they studied one another. Levi kept his large hand firm and never broke eye contact. He worked on what to say to the man.

"Nice to meet you." Except Levi was not so sure. This supposed man of the cloth came across as an overconfident, self-assured prick.

"Well, after a few hours, let's hope you still feel that way," the priest said. "Drew, is the cooler full?"

"Per your orders, I have not opened it since you closed it."

"You're a good man. You passed another test."

Father Paul gripped the bags and went behind the bar toward the walk-in cooler. Drew looked at Levi and shrugged, then bounded after the priest. Curious, Levi left his stool and followed. As he turned past the counter, he paused, as Hannah was at his side. He sensed her warmth and energy, immediately catching his breath. *Pull yourself together, man.*

"Drew, you bought a real restaurant refrigerator?" Levi asked.

"I did. Nothing is zoned out here, and I always said I wanted my own private place, but I figured I could obtain the permits. Then build it. There's also a full-sized kitchen."

"Any chef would love the setup too." Hannah wore a large smile and giggled.

Levi deduced her elation centered more on whatever "freaky shit" existed inside the fridge than anything else.

Father Paul unlocked the padlock to the chain tying the ice locker's handle. The door opened, and they followed the muscular clergyman into the cold.

A slim bald woman with an oversized head lay face up on the floor. Her skin sported a tainted blue color, and her only obvious injury came from a mangled gash where a vacated left arm once existed. Levi assumed she bled out somewhere else, since nothing pooled near her open wound. Her head had swelled as if a basketball was about to pop out of her skull.

Around one of her bulging eyes, Levi detected a thin, dark trail of dried blood. Her cold, empty stare triggered a chill within him. *This poor woman.* He wanted nothing to do with this, whatever the circumstance. He did not want to be implicated in any of it—or, worse, end up like the victim on the floor. Both Hannah and Drew appeared calm. Levi could not comprehend how either of them were comfortable with a corpse in the room. The urge to say something overwhelmed him.

"Drew, that's a dead woman," Levi said.

"Has your friend always been so astute?" the priest asked.

Levi clued to keep his mouth shut but lacked such an ability.

"Why is she here? What's wrong with her head? Have the police been called? Did y'all do …"

The priest gave him a stern look and took a deep breath before he spoke in a calm tone. "No police. We couldn't report the death because I needed to examine her first. As you duly noted, we need to see inside her head. Also, did anyone button up the front yet?"

"Yeah, I don't remember her head being this big when we brought her in," Drew said.

"It wasn't."

"Come on, Levi." Hannah motioned for him to follow her out the door.

"Drew, you know I always have your back, but I'm out."

"It's a new moon, Levi. You'll never make it back to the highway before dark. You're not safe in any vehicle. Out there alone in a car with those things would be far worse than staying here," the priest said.

"Things? Things attacking people in cars at night? Ripping off body parts to where they lack blood? Are you saying vampires exist?"

"Don't be juvenile, Levi. I'll explain more after the exam. Please go lock up."

Levi lost his focus as Hannah grasped his hand, pulling him toward the refrigerator's exit. Her warmth heated his whole arm. A flare blossomed in his chest as if he'd taken a shot of whiskey. Without another thought, he followed her through the door.

"Hannah, I already took care of the back," Drew called out as the two went to fasten down the establishment.

He stayed silent until they reached the main floor, when his overloaded emotions overtook him. In the last twenty minutes, he had touched and conversed with Hannah more than at any other point in the past forty-five years. All of the previous moments combined did not equal this amount of time. His forever crush treated him like a real person, and with all of that, he was unable to let any thoughts about the dead woman in the freezer go. Between both extremes, hyperventilating seemed sensible.

"Hannah, what's going on?"

"I'll explain as we secure the bar. You go close the front. I'll get the floodlights."

By the time he walked out the entrance, the barn's exterior had brightened, the surrounding ground like a Friday night football field. Levi took in the blend of electric lights with the fading sunlight. He enjoyed the view of a good sunset, and this one's beauty held a splendor of exploding orange and red rays, allowing for dusk to have a colorful hazy, dusty hue. Except this time, the setting sun might be the worst thing to happen. He closed the doors to the external world. Hannah arrived to slide the bolt and bound the lever with a padlocked chain.

She moved with assembly line-like efficiency. Her every step contained a slight hop, and each time Levi peeked at her, her radiant smile caused him to grin in response. He found it odd about the lack of creases around her eyes. *She really hasn't aged.*

"Let's check the side exit," she said.

Once they verified the locked door, they set the alarm and made their way behind the bar, where Hannah opened a laptop. Her ease with the machine was evident. She pushed several keys and appeared to review more than cameras. He did not understand anything about computers other than the games on his phone. As a welder, he never needed one. Along with all her activity, she brought up a security camera dashboard showing eight different views.

"You can toggle back and forth and see another group." Hannah clicked the mouse to demonstrate. Her enthusiasm came with a ton of energy.

Is she hyperactive?

Her excitement did register with Levi. "Are you going to explain more?"

"Are you?" she asked.

"What?"

"What answers do you want, Levi?" She paused with her eyebrows raised. "Are you sure you want to know?"

"What are you talking about?"

"I think you do." She angled in close to him, her eyes staring into his.

"No, I don't."

She leaned back. "Maybe you do." Her eyes pierced through his, then she shook her head, offering a slight frown. "Maybe you don't."

Levi's lack of a reply frustrated him. His tongue grew too fat, leaving him with the continued issued of not speaking well. *Did she just lean in to me? Does she know how I feel? Is she interested? No way, that's not within the realms of any possibility.*

"Not exactly." Even to his ears, his response was flat and unconvincing. Drew must have told Hannah something. No explanation existed for her acting this way. Plus, they never talked with one another until now. On one hand, he could count all the times they spoke to each other. Now with her recognition about his crush on her, it added to his growing concern about the evening. Hannah or no Hannah, he needed to do something about the woman in the freezer. "I need some sort of a clue about all this."

"A clue?" She chuckled. "In short, the priest discovered something. He tracked a few disappearances around the bayou, and now, he thinks he found the cause. If he's correct, then tonight's the night."

She started back to the others.

"Hannah, you've told me nothing."

"Bullshit, I told you everything. Let's get back to the fridge to see if the priest is right."

She headed back behind the bar, stopped, grabbed his hand, and pulled him along. He thought of the kids trailing after Willie Wonka in the Chocolate Factory. Just like those kids, he was inferior to his guide in a strange new world. Unlike them, he lacked the golden ticket.

"Come on. I don't want to do any of this without you."

Dumbfounded, he complied and went.

Any thought about the corpse in the cooler worried him beyond reason. But at this moment, he forced his apprehension away as he decided to go to the greatest imaginable lengths to be next to Hannah. If this meant observing a dead body, so be it. Any chance to be in the same room with her. This time, he needed to grow up, no more averting eyes and hiding behind teenage fantasies. Ignoring anything about her was not an option. By the time they reached the freezer door, he'd pushed aside any inhibiting factors from his youth, he'd committed himself to her.

"Is it safe?" she asked.

The muffled response offered no clarity for Levi, and Hannah let go of his hand. She motioned for him to follow her.

When Levi entered, Father Paul and Drew were hunched over something. Both duffle bags lay open, along with the dead woman's head. Levi took note that the eyes no longer bulged. He expected blood everywhere, but very little existed. The trail of red tears and the dried portion near her ears were the only true evidence of any bodily fluid.

Hannah peered over the priest's shoulder. She hurried from the chamber, winking at Levi as she passed him. Her expression still maintained an excitable happiness. Levi did his best to look at what the other two men examined. Something resembling a baby, yet it didn't quite look right.

"I've got a container," Hannah said when she returned.

Levi jumped as she spoke. He hoped no one registered the movement as he eyed the stainless steel canister she carried. To Levi, it resembled an oversized thermos, except the lid appeared to open the entire width of the capsule.

"Levi," Father Paul said, "come over here. You need to see this. As does everyone."

The priest sounded like a teacher. An image flashed through Levi's thoughts of the priest viewing them as little children at vacation bible school. Levi did as instructed and huddled beside the rest where the priest stood with an extended metal pointer. The tip of the slender rod touched the top of a small head belonging to what resembled an infant-sized birdlike creature.

"Though the nose resembles a slim beak and the hands appear to be talons, make no mistake, this is not an earthly avian critter. Check out the eyes." The priest reached down with a gloved hand and pulled up the eyelids. "Instead of white, they are gold encompassing another circle of amber, which surrounds a green iris enveloping a darker green pupil.

"Also note there are no feathers or hair of any kind. This is a fetus. The skin is almost translucent and void of color. However, when these things become adults, they turn copper and are very much metallic in appearance. They grow to have a prominent forehead with a slim nose; except, from the profile, it's a very pronounced beaker." From his broad grin, Father Paul appeared amused by his description. It might have been infectious to Levi, yet the woman's corpse was too much for him to find humor.

"Additionally, they are bipedal, with four toes on each foot, but no obvious right or left other than location. The adults attain about nine feet tall. Also note there is no discernible gender, nor anywhere to excrete waste."

The metal tip of the baton drew Levi's eyes near the groin area. Father Paul collapsed the pointer, grabbed the tongs to pick up the critter, and placed it into the open container. Hannah sealed the capsule tight, and Father Paul looked around the small group with his brows up as if he anticipated a question or two.

"So they don't piss or crap?" Drew asked.

The priest nodded, tilting his head. "Not in the manner we understand it. Also, they may use vocal sounds, hand signals, or possibly even telepathy to communicate. Beware of telepathy."

"What the hell does that mean?" Levi asked. None of this made sense. He just wanted a beer, and now he was trying to process the information presented to him. From the priest, to the creature, and now some sort of ESP, Levi needed to scream. The bar was cool, the dead woman wasn't, and this priest's descriptions left Levi with more questions than answers. The man of the cloth was becoming quite a pain and one which smarts the ass like a final nerve ending.

"It means keep your wits about you."

Levi didn't understand. None of this made sense.

"What about the woman?" Levi asked.

"Unfortunately, she's a victim. Probably got lost and these suckers found her." The priest remained unmoved, with a set jaw and upward brows.

"Can't you do anything for her?"

"No. Once the soul's out, that's it." The priest shrugged with his hands up.

Levi's eyebrows furrowed, and his mouth pressed to a thin line. He motioned toward the corpse. "Seriously, no word of comfort. Any words of reception by angels? Anything?"

The priest said, matter-of-factly, "I gave her a fairly good autopsy, and when we leave the body at the morgue, I will provide my findings for the coroner. Everything relating to her actual death, of course. I will not include the discoveries on the fetus and my theories of what type of creatures can be found out here."

"Well, that makes total sense," Levi said with a sneer and sarcastic tone. "Whatever we do, don't warn anyone."

"People as a group can't handle the truth or honest scientific evaluations," the priest retorted.

"Are you a holy man or a scientist?" Levi asked the priest. His inflection condescended to disrespect.

"The best holy men are indeed true scientists."

"I'm beginning to question the *holy*." Levi softened his last word but emphasized it with a soft breath. His fist clenched, ready to throw a punch.

"You want to be on my side or theirs? Middle is not an option." Father Paul still maintained his relaxed stance and flat voice. He didn't offer Levi any sign of remorse or regret.

Levi compared knowns to unknowns. He wanted to choose something else. The limited opportunities came contrary to the country where he lived. One that contained so many supposed freedoms, leaving him in an odd way of having two choices with only one viable advantage. The decision reminded him of church, always picking a side. He did not care for the man, and after running through the complete litany of available options, Levi had no alternative.

"Yours."

"Good. Also, your observation is correct. My calling changed since I first donned the cloth. Drew, reach in the bag and grab the club."

"This?"

"That's the one."

"Is that a macuahuitl?" Hannah asked.

Father Paul appeared astonished and grinned at Hannah like a proud parent. "No, the Aztecs copied it using obsidian instead of the rock on this big stick. This is Mayan. It has three sides of black stone. Except, this ore is not obsidian or any other known substance on Earth."

"Are you saying this bat is from another planet?" Drew asked.

"No, I'm saying the rock on this club is an unknown substance on Earth."

The priest paused as he sized up the ornate cudgel. He appeared to admire the detail. Trailing his finger along the designs, he hesitated over the black stones as he rotated the club. It was as if the man still wanted to learn about the thing.

"Are there two or three more of these in the bag?"

Both Levi and Drew searched the carryall.

"Two," Levi said.

"Okay, then I'll also take one of the daggers. Those are probably at the bottom. Drew, I want you at the side door after I exit. Hannah and Levi, you monitor the cameras, and once I am at the edge of the light, go ahead and flip off the spots. Wait fifteen minutes and turn them on."

"Are you sure this is the best option?" Hannah asked as Drew handed the priest a knife.

"I'm the only one who's seen them, and if my theory is correct about their origins, I should be fine with these two weapons." The priest smiled and held up his items.

Levi was unconvinced about the *best option*, but the safest place would be by the monitor; at least he hoped. He believed Hannah understood something of what was going on and her knowledge might be worth standing near. Though he did have a long list of many reasons why he wanted to be adjacent to her.

"What are their origins?" Levi asked.

"Mayan, so, not of this earth."

"What?" Levi shook his head. *Bullshit.*

"What am I doing at the door?" Drew asked.

"Let me in and only me. Reset the alarm when I go out and hold that stick ready to swing."

Drew nodded with a concerned look and appeared as if he suddenly became not so comfortable with everything happening.

"Listen, these creatures have cut the electricity several times. You have solar power with battery backup and a propane gas generator to maintain the lights. They hate light for whatever reason. It is our best defense. So keep the club up and be prepared to whack anything other than the three of us."

The priest exited the door and shut it before anyone responded. Drew turned to Hannah and Levi without performing any of the priest's requests and shrugged. The door opened. The priest stuck his head in through.

"Besides, you'll be safe as kittens if you lock the door and set the alarm. Plus, you need to be a lot faster with that club."

The cleric closed the door. Drew mouthed at Hannah and Levi, *what the fuck?*

"He's going out into the property now." Hannah maintained her vigil at the laptop, her eyes glued to the screen.

Levi followed her lead and did the same. Father Paul stood in the yard. The man seemed to study the sky for a bit, then peered back at the cameras. He waved and moved forward, disappearing into the darkness.

Crazy. Levi glanced at Hannah as she switched off the outside lights.

He struggled not to stare at Hannah. His fascination with her continued as he noted she wore no perfume, or at least nothing he picked up. She'd donned little makeup. *And how in the world doesn't she have crow's feet?* When he did not focus on her, he measured himself. His pudgy hands, his belly, as well as his clothes—none of it added up to her standards. *What are those, anyway?* He aspired to appreciate her desires and to understand what she wanted in a partner. He stared at his hands some more; his nails needed trimming. *I'm such a slob.*

The rafters above him contained many layers of Edison lights. The incandescent string lights lit the whole top of the barn, and in some way, he wished they would distract him from Hannah. They didn't.

Levi angled his head toward her. He remembered hearing about her earning multiple degrees over the years, and he wondered about her areas of study since she could identify something from an extinct civilization. Knowing he should monitor the outside cameras, he renewed his occasional glimpse of her. Her eyes caught his, and he made himself view the darkened yard.

"Has it been fifteen minutes yet?" he asked.

"Around thirty-seconds," Hannah said.

"Oh." *I'm such an idiot.*

Levi sustained his uncomfortable stare at the laptop screen. He viewed nothing but still concentrated. The void lacked any sort of reason to continue his sentinel state, but it did keep him from staring elsewhere. Still, peering at the darkness allowed the time not to pass. The waiting took forever. His mind wandered from thought to thought. After a few moments, his sight aligned with the two unfinished pints on the bar. *Should I finish one?*

His attention returned to Hannah, and he wondered if she ever married. She never had a boyfriend in school here, except that was not saying much. In reality, most nearby options were a lot like him. She must have found somebody during her time away.

A slight high pitch caught his attention. *My ears? But that isn't right, ringing?* He peered around. *What's that?* Nothing was out of place. *Over here?* The noise seemed odd but not overwhelming.

It sounded familiar but muffled, like coming from a closed room. Suddenly, he stood in the hallway. A door existed at the end.

He needed to go down the passage, but something else forced him toward the door. To the sound. He must do something. No matter what, something wanted him on the other side. It was imperative for him to reach outside. Nothing should stop him from going on the other side. He should be outside. Yes, outside. *Outside.*

Hannah's image popped into his head. Something about outside, something for Hannah. He must go outside. The answer related to her. *Yes, outside.*

Hannah grasped his arm, startling him from his goal. He loved her touch. Except her fingers dug into his bicep, almost drawing blood. The tunnel vision evaporated. The thought of going outside vanished, and his head buzzed.

The love of his life stood in front of him, moving her mouth as if she spoke to him. Nothing auditory reached him. *How strange?* Levi lowered his brows and crinkled his nose as if he had a question.

She waved her arms in his face. Her eyes were huge as she yelled silently at him. Hannah cupped his cheeks. Her eyes stared deeply into his. She leaned close to him, where a full sensation pressed on his lips. Her lips. Levi tingled within.

He moved in response to her kiss. The touch of her soft mouth on his own. The sudden loss of her warmth followed by a slap across his face ended the most wonderful experience of his life. His cheek stung as if a swarm of wasps tagged it.

"Shit! What was that for?" he asked.

"Seriously? You were on your way outside, weren't you?"

What in the hell is she talking about?

"Remember what the priest said?" She answered his question before he asked. She nodded. "Remember beware of telepathy?"

He recalled the statement. However, he was not under a trance. *Was I?* Nothing made sense. "In what world would I know what that meant?"

"Hear the alarm?"

Now that she mentioned it, a high-pitched sound rang in his ears.

Hannah continued, "We lost Drew. Hear the alarm?"

"What?"

He looked at the door. Drew was missing. His heart sank. The squelch annoyed him, and it helped to bring his thoughts into becoming more his own.

"Apparently, you were both hypnotized or whatever, so he went right out the door," she said.

"Flip on the lights."

"No, we have about two minutes left. You go to the door and keep your mind clear."

"I don't have a club."

"He dropped his at the door."

Levi trotted over and turned the lock. He studied the alarm. This belonged to Drew. Understanding his friend the way he did, Levi typed in 1234. This worked; the squelch stopped.

Away from the safety of inside the bar, Drew did not stand a chance. Levi faced some grave choices. First, he picked up the bat. From the initial grip, it seemed too solid to lift. He lacked the confidence he could pick the thing up. The heaviness evaporated. His view changed and now struggled to accept how the weightless object could be a weapon. Especially one used for blunt force damage. The tool didn't matter; his buddy needed help. Levi flexed his shoulders and gripped the Mayan bat tighter as some panic began to form within him. *What's next?*

"What phone will the security company call?" Levi asked.

"None, there's no service."

He reset the alarm. His worries solidified for Drew. Somewhere on the other side of the door, Drew fought for his life. He hoped Father Paul found Drew and everything was okay. Somehow, Levi believed this not to be the case. This was Shoal Point; hoping for the best was a fool's quest.

As Levi continued his tight grip on the club, he envisioned what should be done if the door opened. No matter what came through, he made up his mind to beat it into oblivion, including the priest. *Priest my ass.* He'd give Drew a pass. *Drew would've already been on the other side searching for my dumb ass.*

He reached for the door handle and peeked back at Hannah. Her eyes stared straight at his. *I need to go.* Hesitation took hold as he pondered his next step, if he ran outside after Drew.

"One minute," Hannah stated.

If he went for Drew, his fate, good or bad, would be that of his friend's. So if the priest found Drew, that made for a good thing. Otherwise, if Drew had a case of larvae head, well, that was the worse scenario. Running out the door screaming and without some sort of plan was not smart; plus, leaving Hannah to fend for herself did not seem right. Though Hannah needed him like a vampire needed sunlight.

I can't leave Drew hanging. Except he would be of more use to her inside than out in the dark against whatever the hell those things were. He stayed put and witnessed her flick the switch.

"Everything is on, and I don't see anyone," she said. She tapped on her keyboard a few times as her brows furrowed down. "Something is happening to the spots."

With the yard lit, Levi decided to attempt a rescue effort. He unlocked the door, coded 1234, and tuned into a swoosh sound coming from Hannah's direction. Before he entrusted another thought, she stood next to him, knocking his hand from the handle. *That was fast.* She rotated him to face her and smacked him across the face.

"We don't have time to screw around," Hannah said. She kept her face stern, making it impossible for Levi to differentiate between her being mad or irritated. He realized it didn't matter. Though the slap wasn't as stunning as her first, she'd hit the same area of his face, thus intensifying the sting. She left him and returned to her spot behind the bar.

After he reset the alarm and locked the door, Levi gripped the club and continued his door-duty. The slaps were relevant along his cheek, but the remembrance of her lips caused him to peek back at her. He became uneasy when he thought how hard she possibly punched. He chastised himself for admiring her instead of working on a plan for Drew.

"Still nothing coming to the door," she said. "Another one just went out. Looks like they are throwing something at them. There goes another."

Levi rushed to the monitor. By the time he neared the screen, only one view remained. Something flashed, and the yard went dark. She toggled to the other eight views and flipped the switch back and forth. Nothing showed.

"You want the club?" Levi asked.

"No, I have a flashlight."

"Will that work?"

She nodded, then shrugged. "It's more of a hope."

"You have another flashlight?"

"Underneath our seats. The bar does have emergency lighting. If the breakers go dead, bright spotlights come on near each door and throughout the entire place. We should be okay."

"Comforting."

"Better than nothing. Maybe we should stand by the door."

They headed to the side entrance. Levi let Hannah take the lead. He peered at her for a few steps, then forced his eyes away. He smiled as he spied the Deluxe Blackhawks Bubble tabletop. The plastic hockey game brought a fond memory to the forefront. *Only Drew.* His eyes watered, realizing his best friend's probable fate.

As they reached their destination, Hannah stared at the door handle. He trained his sight on the same thing, attentive to any movement.

"Maybe we shouldn't wait for the knock," Levi said.

She glared back at him. "Be patient."

"Why wait when you can do? I need to go get Drew."

She nodded. "You realize there is absolutely nothing you could do for him out there?"

Levi shrugged with his head down and shuffled his feet a bit. "No."

"Spoken like a real man." Hannah smiled.

Is that good or bad? Levi managed to give himself a mental high five since he was positive he never did one thing to Hannah in which she offered the slightest smirk toward him other than her being friendly.

The first thump on the other side caused an adrenaline rush. The next two followed in rhythmic succession. Hannah opened the door while Levi readied for combat. A ruffled Father Paul entered with an armless, lifeless Drew.

"Sorry. I fought like hell to save him."

Levi's eyes watered. A sudden surge of emotion from his gut erupted up through his chest, and he choked a throaty cry, trying to hold it all within. Drew inhabited every part in Levi's life, through any day of the week, through any event, being the one constant presence. Now, in a matter of hours, his cohort went from showing off his dream to ending in a nightmare. Everything culminated in Levi's head as he gazed at Drew, who stared ahead, fixated on nothing.

Nothing poured from the exposed gashes where limbs once extended. All blood appeared to have been drained from the body.

Drew's head had not swollen like the woman in the freezer, but Levi deduced this would happen soon. *But where are his arms?*

Father Paul closed the door while Hannah turned off the alarm. He pointed at Drew. "It looks like when they implant the larvae within the skull, instinctually people reach for their head. It's feasible for someone to go as far as scratching their ear off and digging into themselves. So these creatures take an arm; if you continue, then they take the other." The priest paused and added, "Just a hunch."

Levi froze. Drew's dead stare into the abyss captured Levi's attention. Drew's once animated face, which spouted out his dreams and let his excitement flow for the opportunities before him, now held an unmoving stillness for eternity. The washed-out, colorless features of his face made him look more like a mannequin than a corpse.

Levi kept his lips pursed and his eyes cast down, attempting to keep his emotions silenced, but a stream of water crossed his cheeks. Father Paul reached over and clasped Levi's shoulder.

"I get what I'm about to say won't mean much to you, Levi," the priest said. "I thought a great deal of Drew. He's a good man. I may seem insensitive to his death, yet I understand it. I know what's on the other side. Drew's at peace."

Levi studied the priest. He attempted to figure the man out. He was not the kind of guy you listened to on Sunday mornings. The man's torn clothes exposed a partial muscled physique; his boots and jeans were muddied to the knees. He must have gone through hell to bring Drew back.

"I appreciate the words, but not all of us are men of the cloth."

"I don't wear the cloth any longer."

Levi did not follow what he meant by *not wearing the cloth*, and he did not want to debate it. His fight left him as soon as dead Drew returned. He did not care about the priest now. He wanted to go home, drink his weight in beer, and pray this was a bad dream, except for the Hannah parts.

"Doesn't matter. I don't want to end up like Drew. I loved him dearly, but I don't want to die like this."

"Levi, we all end up like Drew." Hannah touched his arm.

"Fair point. I'm not going out the way he did."

"Then don't," the priest said.

It's not like Drew had a choice. Levi stared back at the priest. Maybe he just didn't pick up on this guy's fatherly advice as he should. He wanted to punch Mr. Confident square in the nose just to make a statement.

"It's never that simple," Levi said.

The priest shrugged. "Let's get Drew in the icebox to slow down the larvae growth. Afterwards, I will go back outside and do what I need to do."

"What's that?" Levi asked.

"Eradicate the infestation."

Father Paul lifted Drew with ease and walked to the refrigerator where one autopsied corpse lay. Levi and Drew were both a few inches over six feet and weighed in the mid two hundreds, built on a lifetime of hard work and beer. The priest hauled off Drew's body as if he carried a sack of potatoes. Levi glanced at Hannah as if to plead for help, but she followed the priest, getting the door for him.

Levi reflected on Drew. The overwhelming ache of sorrow rose within him. He never thought about the possibility of being so hollow inside. He turned away, toward the arcade area. He would've loved to have been drinking and playing bubble hockey with Drew.

Hannah and the priest reappeared before Levi thought of anything else. Hannah brought the priest's bags over to the bar. Levi became aware they were focused on him. His introverted ways tended to force an intentional closure of his emotions. But he hid nothing. The tears still flowed from an empty heart.

"Levi, I'm going outside. You and Hannah stay near the counter. Hang on to the flashlights in case you need them. I'll take a club and dagger. I have no idea how long this will take, but it's quite a while until sunrise. Even then, it will take a bit before real sunlight shows up."

With no farewells, the priest left. Hannah locked the door, set the alarm, then returned to the bar. She sat next to Levi, sitting on the counter. Some minutes passed before they spoke.

"What's left in the bags?" Levi asked.

Hannah jumped down from her perch and rummaged through the packs.

"Looks like a dagger and a club," she said.

"Maybe we should keep those close, along with the flashlights."

"I like the way you think."

Hannah went back to her seat and handed the dagger to Levi as she laid the bat at her side. He dropped his original club underneath the bar.

"Your weapon of choice?" Levi asked as he nodded at her stick.

"Not really, but their metallic skin description sounded tough, so I figured you had the stronger forearms to force the blade through."

The excitement Levi held after he first arrived had disappeared with Drew's death. He grappled with his feelings about Drew. Though Hannah sat to his left, Drew was a real thing in his life and not some teenage fantasy. In his despair, he checked once or ten times to verify she remained next to him. She appeared to be reading cocktail recipes.

He appreciated Hannah's silence. It gave him time to reflect. Something he only ever did with Drew over plenty of brews. He never wanted to be a part of a story or a legend unless it started with being a tad inebriated at the time. Adventuring was not his calling.

He loved his own tales, and all of those included Drew. Their favorite hangout, Bettie's Saloon, was safer than Fort Knox. He had no idea why Drew became muddled with the priest. Levi wondered if Hannah brought Drew into this mess. She came from the area, grew up here, and understood all the crazy crap around town, but he did not want to believe she would do such a thing.

"Did Drew think he was safe with the priest?" Levi asked.

She looked at him and sighed. "No, in truth, the priest warned him not to get involved."

"Then why did he?"

"Because he wanted this bar."

"Was it worth his life?"

"I don't know." She shook her head and shrugged. "Did he feel alive?"

Silence ensued as Levi continued his reflection on his friend's fate. He didn't like it. Neither he nor Drew were first responder types. He held Hannah's gaze. Her confidence astounded him, but she'd always displayed a self-reliance quality. Somehow, she'd defied aging. He remembered everything about her, and he failed to grasp how she appeared as youthful as the day she graduated high school. He did not need reminders of why his heart belonged to her. No one matched her qualities, such as her determination, courage, intelligence, and pleasant demeanor. Though always popular, her niceness prevailed over everything else. She never became full of herself like the pretty people in the movies. Except now, he learned a new quality about her, one he could live without; she was a definite adrenaline junkie.

His thoughts drifted back to grade school, to when he let Drew in on a little secret. One life-consuming classified piece of information he would never do anything about. Even through all the ribbing, talk, and fantasies, Drew never spoke about any of it. Until now, where this became so obvious to Levi, Hannah somehow found out how he felt about her. That bit of news could have only been from Drew. Maybe the thought was to help make a romance happen, but Levi did not need that kind of help. Something like that would never occur with people like himself and her. He wished one more opportunity existed to ask Drew why he betrayed the trust.

All the opportunities after, all the fights they had, Drew could have thrown Levi into the undertow of childhood gossip. Treachery never happened. After a few hours, they would move past their falling outs and were quick to return to being thick as a swarm of summer swamp mosquitos.

Levi allowed his mind to wander through those stupid times, from arguing over who was the best quarterback in the pros to who cleaned fish better. These events were never serious but tended to be hurtful, from their boyhood pride to competitive hormones. At least in adulthood, they'd never had a disagreement. After around twenty-five, they learned to respect each other's opinion. Levi missed him. *What time is it?*

First the question, then a cramp in his side brought him from his pensive state. *Jesus, how long have I been sitting?* From as stiff as his body felt, maybe he'd daydreamed the night away. His bladder screamed and punched him in the gut. He moved slowly but no option existed for waiting. He bounded off the counter.

"I have to hit the head," he said, angling the dagger between a belt loop on his jeans and the small of his back. He took off before she responded.

On his way back from the facilities, he searched the walls for some sort of clock in the bar. He found none and returned to his seat on the counter as he placed the dagger next to him.

"I wondered if you ever went to the bathroom," she said. "I've gone, like, three times since we've been sitting here."

"How long has it been since the priest left?" Levi asked.

"About five hours. Also, your phone doesn't work."

"What?"

"Just after midnight, all the electronics stopped working. Look at the arcade box over there."

A black screen enveloped the standup game. He gazed at the lit-up pinball machine. All the digital score boxes were blank. Anything that should have a readout was dark. He stared at the empty computer monitor. He picked up his phone and turned it off. Levi counted to ten before attempting to turn it on.

"That won't work," Hannah said as she sipped from her bottle of Topo. "Everything you could use to communicate is useless."

"Oh."

"I'm worried about the lights."

Levi became anxious. He thought more about Drew. His friend achieved a dream, but now it all seemed hopeless. Another tear strolled down Levi's cheek from a combination of sadness and the immeasurable fact of never being able to enjoy the Madhouse. He peered over his shoulder toward the refrigerator and contemplated the coolness of death.

Hannah belched, and it jerked him from his daze. She uttered the name Bert in a coarse manner but through the burp. "And Ernie," she said.

Levi grinned, and right then, his lifetime of infatuation became true love. She caught his glance at her. Busted again.

"You still operate a forge?"

How did she know I did metalwork? He wanted to ask her who told her, but he lacked any sense of being inquisitive.

"Welding and creating new parts takes up most of my time, but a majority of the weekends, I get to bang on some metal. Unless I'm wrapped up in a great book."

She smiled with her head still focused toward the floor. "Why didn't you ever ask me out back in school or whenever I was in town?"

"Huh?'

On a normal night, panic would have set in to the point of passing out. Except, in this situation and with the death of Drew, a numbness took over his emotions.

"You've always looked at me like I was someone special," she said. "You never gawked at me as if I were a piece of meat, or gave me the once over, or, worse, a creepy-ass smile. One, two, or all three happen everywhere I go around the world. But not from you. Yet you always ignored my attention."

"More like I froze on any acknowledgement from you." He paused to take a deep breath. "But let's get real, Hannah. You were valedictorian and voted most likely to succeed, homecoming and prom queen, and whatever else ... you had it. Plus, you are educated. I was just there. In fact, I was voted most likely to be present."

She laughed. "You are far more than present." She reached for his hand. "I like big hands. Yours are surprisingly soft. And about my college education, I have three doctorates, Geology, Anthropology, and Archeology. None of that matters. Besides, you've made me curious. I wonder what it would be like."

"About the two of us?"

"No, what it'd be like to be you ... dating me."

Levi appreciated her mischievous grin. "I think you are being nice to me because I just lost Drew."

She shook her head. Before she could voice a response, the lights went out. No emergency beacons came on. The exit signs disappeared. He grasped his dagger and felt around with his free hand for the flashlight.

"Shit, get down and hide," Levi said as he slid from his seat. A crashing noise erupted from the back of the barn. It sounded as if something had broken down a door. The alarm blared. *At least that works.*

A fight was coming whether he wanted it or not. He tried to calm his heart by breathing as slowly as possible. This did not work. Many thoughts rushed his mind, but one was dominant. If a shot at a life with Hannah ever existed, then confronting these things with everything became his only option.

"Let's stand in the middle and keep our backs to one another," Hannah said.

Levi moved near her and angled his flashlight at the refrigerator, where the hallway extended toward the back. He focused on the dark space.

The glitter of the metallic creatures flickered as if multiple disco balls descended on them. The light kept the monsters at bay for a few seconds. Until the illumination dimmed.

"Get ready; mine doesn't work either."

On Hannah's words, Levi clutched the hilt of the dagger with both hands. Her back pressed against his and gave him some sense of security in the dark. On some unknown instinct, he thrust the dagger up high. The blade hesitated on first contact. The edge slid through something, and from the amount of fluid running down the shank onto his arm, he believed he scored a direct hit. At the same time, all the emergency lights came on.

A large, lifeless avian beast lay on the floor with a very visible gash in its chest. Levi looked around the bar. The remaining humanoids attempted to hide from any light. He sprung over the counter and swung into action.

He kept Hannah at least arm's length away as he charged into the alien group, swinging his blade like a wild man. This was his simple attempt to keep her from his upcoming sphere of carnage. Every time the dagger struck, the Mayan monsters fell with no resistance. Once the metal sank into their flesh or grazed them anywhere, they stopped moving and collapsed.

Fluid splashed all around him. His clothes stuck to his body, and he was unsure if he was sweating or covered in their substance. With each swing, his blade became easier to maneuver. It also sliced through their thick derma with ease. The quick quelling of his prey gave him a sense of control, though it seemed the short sword did its own thing, as if it controlled itself. He followed the lead.

On any laceration, large amounts of sapphire liquid spewed into the air like a volcano erupting into the sky, covering large portions of the floor and furniture. Levi discovered this while retagging a few of the downed beasts clumped on the ground. As soon as the edge drew blood, not only did they stop moving but their death came in an instant. Still in his focus, he sliced through many, thrust into more, and hacked his way into the largest cluster.

With each strike, he thought of the woman in the freezer as well as Drew. His imagination led him to the possible countless thousands who were victims of the alien horde. He didn't think about himself.

His dagger carved anything copper. In his peripheral view, Hannah struck blows with her club. It was not as effective as his weapon but worked well with a double tap.

On the last few, as he slashed about, he separated a head while hacking through a neck. That effort was not intentional, but the next few swings evolved into it. Head removal became the easy targets. As the blade cut through, each head would almost pop up instead of falling straight down. They would hover for a second, followed by a plop to the ground and splitting open like a tossed watermelon. The insides came out a bit different, though. It reminded him of fish guts sliding out of a sliced belly, except the stuff was blue.

His arms never grew tired. Not once did he breathe heavy. *The weapon must do all the work.* As he struck the last one, a blue splatter decorated the green felt of a pool table—he thought the mixture of blue and green made a better color. He took note of himself. The sticky fluid coated his limbs and every part of his clothing.

From the carnage around him, it appeared as though a day-long battle had taken place, yet actually, it lasted no more than five minutes. Avian fiends clumped on the floor like raked piles of leaves on a manicured lawn. It occurred to him that nothing had cried out or made any other recognizable sound during the encounter. Not even a wisp of air rushed by his ears as he fought. Everything was as silent as a snowfall on a winter's night.

He realized he was alone. Fear flared up as he dashed to the bar, where Hannah was returning from the dark hallway. He went toward the darkness as if the sword directed him in the general direction.

"All clear," she said.

"This was way too easy."

"Yep."

A large explosion sounded from the back as if the roof collapsed. Levi ran to the sound. He jolted past the cooler, into the kitchen. Another being commanded the presence of the room. The hole in the ceiling told Levi how it invaded.

This one appeared different from the others, and light offered no visible effect. It stood two feet higher than its peers and had long talons the length of Levi's dagger. Silver eyes right above the much wider and shorter nose pierced Levi. He froze. Though conscious, he had no ability to move or blink.

No high-pitched noise existed as it did earlier. This thing completely controlled him. A kiss would not wake him out of this. Everything within him changed as if he became aware of his organs and blood flow. His thoughts floated. He'd never tried anything as far as drugs, except the occasional joint. This seemed way different than exceeding his natural beer limit. Maybe this was why people took shrooms.

With no choice, he studied the being in front of him. It lacked a true color and was luminescent in the well-lit room. He wanted to warn Hannah, but she'd already followed. In an odd way, he became aware of her presence. Her energy, heartbeat, and even her soul, he sensed the vitality of her essence.

However, the savage never moved its focus from Levi. The pair locked their sights on one another. Everything in the room contained a certain amount of awareness for Levi. Though the alien blocked his view, the priest sneaking up behind it came into his senses. The creature cocked its head almost doglike. This sign, Levi understood. A questioned and misunderstood observance. Before it gained an understanding, the priest swung his dagger across the back of the being's head. The alien collapsed, as did Levi.

LEVI AWOKE. He attempted to open his eyes, but his lids failed to respond. His fingers, arms, toes, lips, turning his head—nothing budged. If he breathed, he lacked the ability to tell. *What the hell?* He wanted to freak out but had no way to do so. His heart did not register his panic.

He lacked any idea how long he was out or even where he was now. Maybe he wasn't awake. Sleep paralysis? Nothing in him moved. Through frustration, he became angry. Rage centered in his chest. He pushed at it from within and released the emotion. He sensed many things rattle close to him. *Was that me?*

Before he attempted anything else, someone entered his area. A vision formed. One where he lay on a single bed near several monitors and where Hannah set a bottle of Topo on the table next to him. He focused on the hospital equipment with wires attached to him. The mental picture interrupted itself, though he perceived her next motion to sit on the bed. *Maybe this is a dream.*

Everything cleared. His view became distinct in his mind, as if watching television without using his eyes. Except unlike a movie on a screen, it was a three-dimensional aspect, as if appearing down from the sky. Another angle came from the side. None of his mental views were singular but all at once. In a way, it was too much visual; still, it was the only way to see. The ability to focus on smaller, more detailed things happened as well. Though he did not understand how. The shapes, colors, along with each component of Hannah's face, came into full view from within his thoughts.

"Hi, honey," Hannah said.

Honey?

"It's been a busy week since you blacked out, but Father Paul thinks we should talk to you every day and quite a bit. I will continue to rehash events until I believe you know what happened. So here's the score. As far as your health is concerned, we are still learning. It's like you're hibernating. Father Paul and who he calls 'the nurse' are treating you. There will always be someone in this room with you. At nighttime, I will sleep here. During the day, I will take breaks and read to you."

He heard but not through his ears. Same as his vision, his brain interpreted the noise. A distinct impression of sound waves registered, and from this, he perceived her voice. Like his sight from within, any resonation, he picked up loud and clear. His physical senses were somehow shutdown, yet something else had awakened inside him. The five human senses were in his head but nothing external.

Hannah paused. Levi believed her to be moving around, then in the background, "Unchained" by Van Halen played. *Nice.* He wished for an option to crank it up. Levi realized how much he missed music. She sat next to him again, and he suspected her fingers wrapped around his hand.

His sense was not sensory. All of his abilities were more perception or concept. It existed within a thought. Her touch, sound, and image came alive in his mind and diverged from anything physical. *I'm holding hands with Hannah.* He wanted to smile, though he'd already determined it was impossible. A lifelong dream culminated with their hands intertwined.

"Now for the business side. Drew left everything to you. He had an agreement with Father Paul, which now carries over to you. Now, I'm your assistant, among other things."

A giggle registered, and he gathered she belched. It sounded like she said Bert through her gas expulsion, followed by her saying "and Ernie" after. The happiness and humor in her expression warmed him. His love for her welled inside and discharged, affirmed by a flutter in the machines next to him. Several short beats in rapid succession. His mind pictured her as she scanned the readouts.

She squeezed his hand, and he still did not have the physical sensation. He understood the motion. His desire was to acknowledge her tenderness, but that did not come naturally. However, the start of this was not too bad. Her reading to him every day and sleeping next to him at night, this setup worked as long as he came out of this funk.

Something hung around her neck. A design created from silver. One he recognized, one of his handmade Celtic crosses he'd made for the spouse of his overseas client.

"I figured you liked my gas mishap from the other night. My mother hated it, but my dad thought it was hilarious. Anyway, since I have your attention, you should know Father Paul arranged for a small relationship adjustment.

"He forged a few documents, for financial reasons. Nonetheless, I'm excited with the possibilities. My point is our official big day happened three days before you knew I'd come back to town. Once you're better, then we can go on our honeymoon."

Levi's excitement shot through him. *A honeymoon would be awesome. But she's married. How else would she have the cross?*

Somehow, he focused on his creation and nudged the bottom up. Hannah's hand clasped the piece.

"Was that you?" she asked.

He did it again as she held it. She laughed.

"Amazing," she said. "So the honeymoon sounds good, then?"

He lifted it once. This time she squealed with excitement.

"Can you move anything at all?"

He raised the end twice in rapid succession. She nodded in response, her hand still clutching the piece.

"I guess now you realize your overseas client was me. Sorry for the deception."

He warmed at the thought. She understood more about him than he ever imagined. Levi was elated about the realization.

"Well, now that we're hitched and you are awake, I might just tell you my age-defying technique. Maybe it'll help you heal."

Of course, he'd observed her youthfulness and was not sure if she picked up on him clueing in on her condition, but he was curious.

Now, with them being married, he must find a way back. No way would he let the fact Shoal Point was not known for happy endings settle in his head. *I have to find a way back.*

A twinge of sadness rose as he thought about Drew's big dream. He wondered if his ol' buddy was aware that his own Hannah fantasy became sort of a reality.

gravedigger's

. . .

one – preparation

As Marlene crossed the county road's decaying asphalt, she spotted an older model Tundra sitting alone in the parking lot. None of their regular clientele owned one like this. Very few cars belonged here—this particular make and color was not one of them.

After working almost every night for the last twenty years at Gravedigger's and living across the street, knowing the customers came with the job. She never took a break except when she travelled for a member. Those trips came by reward of the occasional favor. On some of those, she traversed the world, and no matter how wonderful the sights, she preferred to perform her nightly ritual of slinging drinks to the thirsty. She did it every day, even on Christmas.

Being summer now, nights were shorter, the bar stayed open less. The additional hours during Fall and Winter were her favorites. The final weeks of the year allowed for more of the opportune moments from the completion of dusk until the start of dawn.

Gravedigger's was her twenty-four-hour-a-day responsibility. Though family owned, the place became entrusted to her as soon as she hit adulthood. The daily grind of running it, managing maintenance, keeping the peace on rowdy shifts, and vaulting the secrets—all of it remained in her care.

"So, who do we have here?" she asked aloud as she journeyed past the truck toward the graveyard. The hard, red dirt crunched underneath her steel-toed work boots.

From the gate, she saw someone at the back near the recent burials. Plots were still available, but only a precious few. The funeral company side yearned to expand the fenced area, but the Council still debated if they desired more internments than originally planned. The Council made and enforced the rules. She followed them without question, to the letter of their law.

The Council controlled the citizenry of the graveyard. The family company owned the necropolis and the church-turned-bar as well as the surrounding five thousand acres. Her grandfather built a thriving business of funeral homes along with many other enterprises, and her relatives were well adept in running those. She wanted nothing to do with providing any of those services. No, Marlene preferred serving the exclusive.

The call of a red hawk and a fresh cut grass aroma hit her senses like smelling salts. She chastised herself for not paying attention. Bob maintained the manicured grounds. His truck and yard tools were nowhere around. Years ago, he told her the graveyard gave him the creeps. He still did his job, but he always disappeared two hours before sunset. The higher blades of Bermuda on the edge of the nearest monuments confirmed it. He never asked about the bar. She was thankful a lot of people visiting during the day missed the oversized neon sign out front. She figured tomorrow, he would return to complete the trimming.

She waited a few moments, but the person lingered at the grave. Marlene needed to finish her setup in order to open on time.

"I hope they don't stay out there past dark," she said. The uninvited staying in the area after dusk tended to make for stressful nights, as they interrupted the peaceful nature of the place. Her intuition had screamed about her next shift since she'd left the doctor's office earlier in the day. None of that mattered; for now, she had work to do, and she filed the morning announcement away as she reached the entrance.

The weather-beaten doors brought her to a contented state. The mahogany-stained wood stayed sturdy through the years. These things may be worn, but not old. She scratched her boots on the outside mat, knocking away the loose dirt.

The door unlocked as soon as she touched the handle. She pressed down on the brass lever and entered. Her first task was to open the patio on the east side. It also permitted the fading natural light to wander inside. The fresh air blended with the cleaning odors from when she closed at sunrise earlier in the day. She was still alone. No one showed early, and definitely not an hour before. Regular guests arrived after dark. Gravedigger's only opened at night, and the members liked it that way.

two – amends

Ray stood at his grandfather's grave. He regretted visiting here. Without any doubt, he loved the old man, but after a decade behind bars, the last place he wanted to go was somewhere reminding him of his loss. The funeral and afterlife stuff was not what he missed but all the times he could have still enjoyed with the old man. His usual monthly visits ended the day of his arrest, and due to not being able to afford bail, along with the "benefit" of a court-appointed attorney, he spent two years in county lock up with another ten at state. His time in the local pen somehow did not count toward his long term.

He stared at the flat grass-covered ground. Some dry cracks allowed ants to move more freely between above and below. The stone appeared small to him, but his Pops had specified all his earthly post-death desires. The executor and lawyer swore every instruction would be fulfilled. The same one found Ray a do-good legal type who wrangled him out of a wrongful conviction and ended his sentence fifteen years early.

His correctional experience was shit, but he'd adapted. The memories were still too fresh after only getting out earlier in the morning.

He did not have a place to stay. His recent attorney worked pro bono, and after the overturned sentence, Ray was free. No parole. No other court dates. He escaped the judicial system legally. The truck was a loaner, something the do-gooder used for hunting.

"Well, Pops," he said to the gray granite tombstone, "I'm here. I'll wait for the attorneys as you instructed, and tonight, I will go to this crazy church bar after I'm done visiting you. Sorry about not making it out to see you while you were still here."

Tears welled. He loved this man with every fiber of his soul. Now, he spoke to a corpse dirt napping in no telling what. Ray struggled with how the old man could know a graveside visitation happened, but the letter from Pops's attorney specified the old man's awareness. It didn't matter. Ray never wanted to disappoint Pops, alive or dead. Besides, the guilt for not being available at the end would never change. No one should die alone. Ever.

"I wish there was some way to actually chat," Ray added. "I miss you so much, and I hate to say it … you were right."

Ray did have money stashed away in a safe. So when the government closed his bank accounts, he'd still had enough for a retainer. Except his girlfriend took the stash and ran away. He had no idea where, nor did he care, though he'd heard various stories. Pops was spot-on about her.

Enzo, his heist partner, could not assist due to association as well as being arrested himself. Ray never saw his buddy again. On the inside, rumors had swirled around Enzo's disappearance. He bet the body would never be found.

Ray came to the cemetery to honor Pops's specified last wishes and did so out of love. The only reason to do it. Picturing the gold lenses magnifying the gray eyes of an old man with a bushy white mustache and not a spec of hair on top came completely unhindered in Ray's memory. Nothing was ever this clear when he closed his eyes in prison. The old man's smile resonated. For this brief exchange, Ray was thankful.

Still, the old man died alone because of someone's betrayal and greed. Ray never forgave himself for being that trusting. Now, he stood at the memorial of the one he should have paid the most attention to, and as those feelings came to roost on his soul, his shoulders sagged a bit. Only the ones left behind missed the dead. Ray was one of those.

three - the early arrivals

Marlene's favorite time of the day came with dusk. As the sun dimmed, all the electrical illumination triggered automatically, the temp cooled around the old church, and a fog enveloped the property. It meant opening time. The beer signs glowed in their respective brand colors, from the old Budweiser to the newer, colorful Corona offering beach, parrots, and a sunset. The Edison lights strung through the wooden rafters brightened the ceiling, giving it a starry effect. The sign out front would be on, and as the dark crept on the facility, the blue glow of neon would mix with the surrounding red dirt, creating a purplish hue.

She continued behind the bar, humming the last song she heard on her playlist as she stacked fresh pint glasses. Working as a bartender was not a glamorous career choice for most, but those not choosing this path were clueless about the bar's clientele. Things about their lives, their interactions with friends and family, and all their love or hate stories. She wondered if she should share her news.

Hearing someone approach, she guessed the footsteps belonged to the Tundra person. She opened an old, white leather book. One name existed on the page. It appeared they were going to have at least one guest tonight. Marlene faced the man walking toward her. She did not recognize him, so she waited until he sat before she started another task.

"Can I help you?" she asked.

"Maybe." He adjusted himself on the stool. "My grandfather told me to come here. I never knew this was a bar."

"Since seventy-nine."

"I don't remember ever seeing it."

"Well, most people don't see it, especially on a backwoods dirt road."

"Wasn't the county dry in seventy-nine?"

"Not this part."

"Oh."

Marlene did not press him with questions. This was an invitation only establishment, though they allowed the nonmembers to enter. To remain inside, they must be included on the guest list. Once acknowledged and accommodated, a guest enjoyed almost all the perks of membership, yet the uninvited would need to leave. God forbid if they faked being invited. Based on the limited information, she believed he was in the right location.

"So your grandfather told you about Gravedigger's?" she asked.

"He's buried in the cemetery."

"What's his name?"

"Joseph Messina."

"Out at the back, near the woods."

"Yes."

"You Ray?"

"How did you know?'

"Part of my job. It's a private institution. My family owns this old church and the graveyard."

"Your family also has the funeral home? You a Krol?"

"Yes, we do, and yes, I am." She'd never met this man in her life, but he was without a doubt acquainted with the area. "I'm Marlene Krol."

"Hi."

"Why is your name familiar?"

"Maybe my grandfather mentioned me?"

"I don't recall—" she started, then held her tongue, not understanding how much Ray comprehended about the establishment. "He was buried around seven years ago, correct?"

"Yes."

"Didn't you see this place when you went to the funeral?"

"I didn't make it. He told me to come out as soon as I could."

"Overseas?"

"Prison."

Marlene smiled. "Welcome to Gravedigger's."

"Thanks."

She poured some Redbreast into a small glass. "First one's mine."

Since she had an actual customer in the bar, she went ahead and donned the rest of her uniform. Unique for the area but something handed down from her grandfather, it was an average-sized black leather top hat. The topper flared rising up to the crown, making it an old undertaker style. The only difference was the imprinted white skull and cross bones, not like a pirate's but more of a chemist's. She thought it appropriate, being the resident mixologist.

"Nice hat," Ray said.

"Thanks, it was my grandfather's."

"Cool grandfather."

"From my perspective, that's a yes."

"And from mine, that's a no," Alice said.

Marlene managed a smile as she turned toward the woman standing behind her. Alice tended to pop up as soon as the fog enveloped the building. She never had a clue if Alice was going to work the night or party until dawn. Wearing the bar's black t-shirt with the Gravedigger's logo on the right side and "A members only establishment" underneath it indicated she thought of working. Either way, Marlene was glad whenever the woman showed.

Alice embraced Marlene. "When are you going to tell me?"

Marlene broke their hug. "How did you know?"

"Really? You're asking me that? It's been almost two weeks; I've been hoping you'd say something first. Waiting's not my thing."

Before the conversation continued further, Alice returned through the kitchen doors as a party of twenty-somethings entered. Their boisterous nature didn't quite match the ambience this early in the evening. Marlene studied the group, and having acquainted herself with the guestbook for the night, this small mob lacked invitations. Without any recognition of any of them, she surmised they were not local.

"I told you this place was awesome," one yelled out as they grabbed a table in the middle.

"I thought tonight might get interesting," Marlene said under her breath.

four - a whole lot of clanking going on

As Alice entered the kitchen, the sound of crashing dishes added to the cluster of noises.

"Damn it, Camila," Chef said, never looking up from his mixing task, "can you be a bit more careful?"

"Sorry, Chef," Camila responded while running for a broom and trashcan in order to remove the ceramic shards.

"I'll help," Alice said, ignoring Chef. He treated everyone rough at the start of the night. Once the food came out, his demeanor softened and being near him became an actual enjoyable experience.

Alice picked up chunks of the broken dinnerware and tossed them into the trash as Camila swept up the smaller remnants scattered around the main pile. The white particles were easy to spot against the dark-stained concrete of the kitchen floor. It took no longer than a few minutes to get all the pieces put away, and Alice continued with assisting Camila setting up the dishes for serving meals.

She then went and retrieved the colored chalk and display slate before asking Chef what the specials of the evening were.

"Alice," Chef said, "I have no idea how your family always gets some of the finest ingredients delivered to out here in the middle of nowhere, but the freezer and refrigerator are always full, as well as the shelves. The fruit and vegetables are impeccably fresh, and I can think of no finer kitchen to work in ... though I do miss going and picking out my own sources."

"Think of it as ... Nirvana," she said, grinning.

"I do." Chef continued kneading dough.

"However, I do need the specials."

"French Dip, Reuben, and a meat lover's pizza. For dessert, there is red velvet cake, and the appetizer is Calamari."

"Wow, plus the regular menu?"

"Yes."

She searched around the kitchen, and not a soul stood still. They all attended to their duties. She realized Chef, who always preferred to bake, was making the pizza dough and had already prepared the batter for the French Dip as Nanette placed the rolls into the oven.

Alice marveled at how it could be so busy yet still clean. How the stainless steel shined, and as anyone finished one part, they cleaned their area before starting the next. The whole room sparkled.

She glanced down at the empty slate and began her decorative words using the pastel chalk. She would add a few pictures as she went. It was the only art she ever got to do in her life except for when she was a young child. Her mother always insisted she learn to oil paint. It drove Alice crazy at the time. What she wouldn't give for a blank canvas, a nature still, fresh paints, and new brushes. She had the time, but she didn't have the studio.

five - the uninvited

Marlene started cutting limes as one of the new arrivals approached the bar with a credit card in hand. His khakis and loafers were a bit out of place for a jeans and t-shirt kind of establishment.

"Can I get a round of …?" he asked, staring past Marlene as he studied the tap handles. "Do you have any light beer on draft?"

"No," Marlene answered, her lips still offering a smile. "Nothing light in the cooler either."

"Seriously?"

"Yep. Most of the clientele have zero worries for calories, nor would they give a rat's ass about carbs."

"Oh." The young man paused. "How about a couple of pitchers of Modelo and a cranberry-pineapple vodka? I would also like to open a tab. I can grab everyone's IDs to show we are all at least twenty-one." He slid the card across the bar.

Marlene read name and pushed it back.

"Including the skinny brunette?"

He laughed. "She's the oldest of us."

"Listen, Daniel, this is a private place. Members and guests only. We do not accept payment here."

Daniel nodded, then smiled. "Great, we are guests of Joe's."

"Joe who?"

"Joe Smith."

"Are you positive about this or just guessing?"

"We are his guests."

"We have a Joe Smith as a member, but I am certain you are not with him."

"Oh, but we are."

"Everyone who wants to drink will need to stop by and verify they are his guest."

"Okay."

"You understand there is a severe punishment for lying about being invited?"

"What? We have to wash dishes or something?"

"Not so simple. It will be brutal beyond your current comprehension and will be dealt immediately. Dishonesty is punished here. Are you sure you want to declare yourself as a guest of Joe Smith's?"

The young man smiled, his youth and inexperience shining through like a cop's flashlight into drunken eyes. His naiveté made her want to squint. Warning violators in this instance became a necessity. The punishments were too extreme for modern civilization.

True to her own nature, Marlene believed in trying things and pushing boundaries to experience them; it was how she ended up backstage at Metallica, including the afterparty. However, it was very tame compared to the stories from the eighties. She was positive her grandmother hit one of those parties for more than one band. Marlene enjoyed thinking about her headbanging relative.

"Indeed I do," Daniel said with a confident nod.

"Okay, have everyone come to the bar and declare their names as well as about their guest host. Warn them as I have warned you. Then I will have your order delivered."

Daniel returned to his group for the discussion. They all laughed except the skinny brunette, who turned back to Marlene. They held each other's gaze for a few moments. The young woman displayed some level of understanding or intuition. Marlene believed this one would not lie.

"All that seemed way more formal than the way you greeted me," Ray said.

"Well, there's a huge difference between members, guests, and the uninvited," Marlene said, her attention still fixated on the group as she responded.

"I must be on the list, then." Ray took another sip of his drink. "But it's piqued my interest on what happens to the uninvited."

"Uninvited?" Alice questioned as she came from the kitchen and glanced across the tables, looking past the bar. She turned to Marlene. "And I thought it was going to be a quiet night," she said as she dropped her notes on the counter and returned through the doors.

"Lying about the dead," Marlene said, "in any way, about them, anything to do with them, in any manner is severely punished."

"Is Joe Smith dead?"

"As of September 24th, 1854. Interred out back." She pointed behind the church in the direction of the cemetery.

"He's still a member after death?"

"Interment out there guarantees membership forever."

"But how does this work for members like Joe?"

Marlene chuckled, maintaining a smirk. "The more time you spend here, you'll gain a greater understanding of the inner workings of this place, as well as who resides in the graveyard."

"You know all the markers?"

"They're like family to me."

"I might have to get a plot."

"Your grandfather already arranged it."

"Does that make me a member?"

"After you sign." Marlene offered a hand gesture as if she were signing a document made of air.

"Cool."

Two of the uninvited approached the bar.

six – **confirmations**

Two people left Daniel's table. It was impossible for Ray not to stare at them. They appeared as something from a fashion magazine. He read plenty of those in the joint. The broad-shouldered man wore a tight pullover, maybe a Polo, Ray couldn't tell from this angle. However, the young's man biceps rippled every time he moved his arms. Ray bet the guy pumped iron for two hours right before arriving at the bar.

The woman's curves around the hips made her short shorts shorter. Ray figured all men took heed of her, most of all those fresh out of prison—no way in any part of the universe was he going to ignore anything about her. A basic floral aroma accompanied her, and Ray picked out a definite jasmine scent. He did his best not to stare as he took in more than was necessary. Her tight white fitted tank top removed any need for imagination. The crisp night air exposed the woman's lack of undergarments. Ray became uncomfortable. Though he glanced at the two, Ray took note that both people were unaware of his existence as he sat with his drink in hand.

"We're supposed to tell you we are guests of Joe Smith?" the young lady asked.

"Yes, only if you are an actual guest," Marlene said with a flat tone.

"Apparently, we are," the woman responded, her last two words coming out as a sigh. Her statement came off as annoyed.

Marlene shook her head with disapproval. "You either are or you are not. And here, when you say you're something you're not, punishment is swift and severe. Did Daniel mention that part?"

Both twenty-somethings nodded.

"And you are?" Marlene asked.

"I'm Harper, and this is Brad."

They slapped their driver's licenses onto the counter.

"I don't need those," Marlene said. "And you are positive that you are guests of Joe Smith?"

"Evidently," Harper said. "Daniel knows him or of him. We are with Daniel."

Marlene kept a stern expression. She opened the small white

leather-bound ledger, followed by a red one. Ray peeked over the bar but didn't see anything legible. Three thin volumes were visible, all untitled, the third being black.

"Harper Kennedy and Bradley Johnson?" Marlene asked as if she read the names from the red book.

Brad and Harper glanced at one another with confused expressions.

"Listen," Marlene started with firmness in her voice, "you don't have to go along with Daniel, and all friendliness aside, there are severe penalties for lying. You both need to understand there is no plausible deniability here."

"Plausible what?' Brad asked.

"It means you can't pin this all on your buddy Daniel over there. If you say you are a guest but aren't, you will be punished just the same."

"We're guests," Brad said.

"You sure?" Marlene asked one more time.

"Listen, lady," Harper said, "back off on the *Law and Order* shit. Ditch the drama." She flipped her hand up as if to wave her off and added an eye roll.

"First off," Marlene said with a flat tone, "I'm no lady, young, old, or royal, and second, yes, there is; punishments are no slap on the wrist or worked off with trivial labor. They are harsh and long lasting. In some cases, forever. It all depends on you." The bartender paused. "And if you ever address me like that again, one of the bouncers will toss you in a place you can never get out of. Understood?"

Both nodded, though Harper didn't seem as exuberant as she did when they first approached the bar.

Ray studied his new favorite barkeep. Her dark hair and eyes did not match any of the other Krols he met over his time running through this area. They were all blond, blue-eyed, and tanned. Every one of them appeared as if they surfed in Southern California for a few years. Marlene's skin came about as pale as it could. Her thin nose matched her chin and her high cheekbones, completing a more exotic appearance. Ray became a bit more curious, watching the woman as she handled the two unwanted guests.

"Okay," Marlene said, "it's yours, the whole forever, all yours."

The two walked off, leaving Alice, Ray, and Marlene.

"So the list grows," Alice said, peering around Marlene, staring down at the pad.

"Yes, it does."

"That serious?" Ray asked.

"Yes," Marlene replied, "and as you sit here through the night, you will understand more."

"Well, I'm definitely interested now."

The line formed next to Ray. The first handed his ID over to Marlene.

"I'm Ted Nguyen," he said, "and I'm also a guest of Joe Smith's. And to keep this short, Harper told us you said the penalty was severe for lying about being a guest. We all accept that."

"You sure?" Marlene asked.

They all nodded, and the remaining three offered their IDs as well.

"I don't need any of these," Marlene said without touching them.

"I'm Regina and a guest of Joe Smith."

"I'm Shelley and a guest of Joe Smith."

"I'm Vickie and a guest of Joe Smith."

"I'm Nick, Joe Smith's guest."

Ray leaned forward onto the bar as far as possible, peering at the names on the open page of the red book. Ted Nguyen's name, along with a Victoria Zapata, displayed in small and faint black letters compared to Nicholas Foreman, Shelley Adams, and Regina Rosenberg. Those were in bold and thick red letters. Each written as a signature and all in different styles.

The only person who had anything red was Alice. This was the color of chalk she used for the lettering on the slate. That would never write well in the book. Ray sat back on his stool and pondered how bad it would be for these kids. Though they were adults to the world, they were way too juvenile for something as benign as drinking beer for free. He speculated on how the names were added to the books. Alice only glanced up from her work to see which twenty-something spoke.

"Once the last one of you comes over, then Alice will bring Daniel's order over."

"I'll be your server tonight," Alice said with no smile or warm expression, nor did she avert her attention away from the board on which she wrote.

The group left the counter.

"They have no idea," Marlene quipped, maintaining her focus on those returning to their peers. They were five picnic-style tables away. The uninvited had joined two together, placing chairs at either end. "But they do make themselves at home."

An elderly couple arrived and sat at a table near the bar. Ray glanced at them, since he picked up on some commotion behind him. He thought for a second the twenty-somethings moved.

"Well, I'll be," Alice said. "I haven't seen them in a few decades."

"So you knew them when?" Ray asked.

"Don't be tacky, Ray," Alice said, maintaining her smile. "I'm just happy I have more than the party group awaiting their sentencing." She took off to her new guests.

"Are they members?" Ray asked, indicating the recently arrived couple.

"Most certainly," Marlene said, "but they haven't been around much."

"Hi, I'm Fiona," another woman said.

Ray never heard her approach the bar. Background noise did not exist yet, so it was quiet enough where anyone could hear everything coming and going. She was so slender, and with her pale skin, she appeared as a waif of a girl. Describing her as thin was an understatement. Her eyes were big and amber in color, but her long hair embodied a natural curl, allowing some texture, the thickness and shape giving off vibes of being produced by an expensive stylist. However, with her lack of makeup, her overall appearance was that of a thirteen-year-old who threw on some jeans and a t-shirt before heading out the door and didn't have to do anything to her natural hair. His old girlfriend longed for that kind of hair and spent thousands on trying to achieve it. The thought brought back memories, and Ray presumed some of the money she took went to the endeavor of maintaining an over-expensed style.

"It's a pleasure to meet you, Fiona," Marlene said. "Are you the same as your group?"

"No, I have no clue who Joe Smith is, and they probably don't either, though I don't know for sure."

"You don't?"

"Daniel sounds pretty sincere about it." Fiona shrugged. "We went to college a couple of hours south of here and met up for a five-year reunion. One thing led to another, and we ended up here. I didn't realize it was members only."

seven - the non-confirmation

Marlene stared at the woman's eyes, but she was at a loss for reading Fiona's. The large orbs displayed an innocence, but Marlene picked up on a struggle of experience behind those pupils. She sensed something within Fiona, fighting hard to win, but what it fought for as well as what it was, Marlene could not determine. However, the spiritual virtue explained to some extent on how the group ended up here. How they found the building and recognized it as a bar. There may have been other connections, but Marlene was sure Fiona led the party here.

"So," Marlene elongated the word, "you're not a guest of Joe Smith's."

"I'm not. I'm with them, but I don't know Joe Smith. I'll go if I need to."

Marlene glanced down at the books. She opened the white one. No new names were written on either pad.

"Not just yet." Marlene said without looking up. "So you aren't ratting them out?"

"I'm a fan of mob movies. Bad things happen to rats, and I was raised not to lie."

"Most of us are brought up that way."

"My mom was strict when it came to lying. She seemed to think maintaining a sense of freedom hinged on being truthful."

"Your mother taught you well."

Marlene maintained her focus on both books, then glanced up quickly at the woman standing on the other side of the bar. She evaded her eyes this time. Something deep inside Marlene wondered if they were kin to one another. Plus, she worried why the woman did not appear in either book. Marlene found it curious and bizarre.

"Do I need to go?" Fiona asked.

The name Fiona Grant appeared on the guest list. Written as the person's actual signature.

"No," Marlene said, "but you have to remain here at the counter. You'll be my guest. Your friends are on their own."

"For real?"

Marlene nodded. "Welcome to Gravedigger's. First drink's on me. What'll you have?"

"Margarita?"

"Coming right up."

Marlene snagged a margarita glass and moistened the edge with a lime wedge. She turned it upside down, placing it in a dish filled with salt, turning the glass a few times and setting it down on the bar. As she set the prepped glass down with her left hand, she grasped a copper cocktail shaker with her right. She ran it through the ice bin, then reached in the well, gripping a bottle of 1800 Cristalino. She poured it into the cup along with triple sec and some lime juice. Marlene capped it and shook.

She glanced at Ray and Fiona with a smile. "The juice is squeezed fresh."

Marlene stopped shaking once the copper frosted over. She poured and served the drink to Fiona, who took a sip.

"Oh, this is good."

"Thanks."

Marlene took a pint glass and rinsed it as Alice returned to the bar. She shook the glass a few times, removing the bigger droplets, and reached for a distinctive red handle.

"Whiskey sour and Bud on draft … I'll get the water," Alice said as she emptied the ice scoop into a fresh glass.

Marlene pulled the tap beholding a figure of a Clydesdale at the top. She angled the receptacle and then straightened it as the amber contents filled past the label. After the pour, she grabbed another copper cup, a bottle of bourbon, and began her mix. Alice put all three drinks on a tray. Before she delivered to her newest table, she glanced at Fiona.

"Is the order set for the uninvited?" Alice asked Marlene.

"It will be by the time you serve that order."

Marlene had the two pitchers ready, accompanied by a stack of glasses. She was mixing the cranberry drink.

"Awesome … they should get a little out of this prior to their hell."

eight - filling in

The noise level subtly increased. The tables were about half full. Marlene spoke with a couple of other ladies who wore server aprons along with the black t-shirts, one with the slogan of *Get Your Spirits Here* and the other, *Be Wicked Free*. Something about spirits rang true. Ray realized this place might be something other than a regular bar. Though the architecture maintained an old country style, it was indeed large. He did not walk around and take note of the entire building, but it had been enhanced over the years. It was impossible to tell if the Krols created the expansion when they opened or if this happened through the years of the church. He assumed since they were toward the back, they presently were set in the pulpit area. For the age of the structure, he doubted there was a baptistry inside. However, if there had been one, it would have probably been turned into a hot tub.

Ray studied the room. The crowd was diverse in cultures, race, and age. Everyone's eclectic fashions varied to the point of not making sense. Some people dressed in clothes from the early 1900s, others in old west styles, some in Sunday suits or dresses, and several in jeans and t-shirts. The variations in the headwear stood out from cowboy hats to trucker caps. Gender did not matter; almost everyone wore one. The only ones without anything on their heads were the uninvited plus himself.

Behind the bar, filled pitchers of beer lined the counter with pint glasses in stacks of five next to them, Marlene made drinks, but no one wrote down orders or gave them to her verbally. He surmised most servings were for regular clientele.

Fiona sat to his left, and a middle-aged man took the stool to the right. Marlene placed a shot glass in front of the new patron and poured from a dark-brown bottle. It appeared old, the label showing an old-style picture of a multi-storied building from Nun's Island with Persse's Ltd Galway Whisky written across the top of it. He did not recall ever seeing a label with a picture on it.

Some of the safe manuals Ray read over the years had something similar on their front pages, even down to the font, but those safes were manufactured in the 1800s. He imagined the current pour from Marlene was at least a hundred dollars in any other place. Ray was glad this was all free. Marlene put pint of red ale next to the shot.

The man swallowed his whisky, followed by a long swig of ale. "Now that's worth the price of admission," he said with his eyes never leaving the beer in his hand.

"Well, Ray, you want another?" Marlene asked.

"I think I'll try the red," Ray said, pointing at the ale being consumed. "It sounds divine."

"Well, I wouldn't say anything holy about it ... but it is pretty damned good. You might take a shot too," the man said.

"Don't know if I can afford shots."

"It's free, Ray."

"You know who I am?"

"Of course. Marlene said your name." The man chuckled as he took another swig.

Marlene set the ale in front of Ray. He sniffed the toasted caramel aroma and took a sip. The full-body flavor of the same scent flowed across his tongue, bringing a smile to his face. It had been too many years since he'd had a beer, and this one was perfect.

"Enjoy," Marlene said and returned to a well station.

"So, Ray," the man said, "you're a guest of Messina's?"

"Yes, how did you guess that?"

"I'm familiar with the list behind the bar. I run the Council. I'm Julian."

"Oh, Marlene mentioned something about that. She said her family owns the land and business, but the Council makes the decisions."

"She's correct."

"Asshole," Alice said as she walked by, heading to one of her tables.

"Going a little young today?" Julian asked in the direction of Alice. He smiled at Ray. "Never mind her … she's my ex."

Comparing the ages between the two, there was at least a thirty-year difference. Based on Alice's age, they could not have been together long, or they started early, which would mean the guy next to him would have been incarcerated. Either way, from recent life behind bars, Ray never considered to glance over his shoulder at Alice. Whenever someone mentioned anything about anyone, the last thing you did was peek. Guilty eyes made you a target, and that easily happened when somebody said something. Only the best poker faces could pull off peering around without getting busted. He lacked such a skill. Besides, *never make eye contact*. For now, he focused on how well his beer tasted.

"How much did Marlene tell you about guest privileges?"

"She said the first drink was on the house."

"That's true."

"Not long after, a group came in."

"The interlopers."

"The what?"

"The uninvited." Julian took a swig. "It's not an issue they came in, but they lied about being a guest. Plus, who they're a guest of. So their one lie became two. I can't help them."

"Can anyone?" Fiona asked from the other side of Ray.

"Only if they fess up before Joe Smith gets here."

"That's all they have to do?" Fiona asked.

"There's more, but that's a start."

"I thought Joe Smith was interred out back," Ray stated.

"Aren't most of us?" Julian asked.

Ray hung on to the odd question. Possibly, the gent meant they had plots out there so they were already committed in that sense.

"What happens when Joe Smith arrives?" Fiona asked.

"I don't know, but Joe's not nice."

Ray focused on Joe being buried out back, then entering the place. Gravedigger's was definitely different, but that would be a tad much. He struggled to fathom how someone dead since the middle 1800s would show up. His interest piqued more about what could happen next.

nine – wondering

Her old man sitting at the bar was not in Alice's plans, and she damned sure was not about to let the old cudgel ruin her night. Him and his underhanded comments reached deep within and tugged on every part of her fiber. One day, she would figure something out to fire back at him, but she struggled with pulling off that feat prior to their time here, and certainly after.

Alice delivered all of her orders and started taking next rounds. When she stared into the faces of the uninvited, the old mother in her began to pour out. She wanted to scream at them to set their priorities straight. They needed to quit trying to game every system and learn when to play by the rules.

"If any of you are feeling weird about saying you're a guest of Joe Smith, go up to the bar and talk to your friend up there."

"Feel weird?" Brad asked.

"Yeah," Alice said, "weird, as in your conscience is getting to you, a sense of dread or impending doom hovering over your shoulder."

The whole group turned their heads toward Fiona. Only one spoke.

"I don't ever feel that way," Harper said.

"Well, as the adage goes … the world is made for people who aren't cursed with self-awareness," Alice retorted. "Another round?"

"Yes," Brad said. "And can we get another server?"

"Of course. It's your funeral."

Alice left the table. When she returned to the bar, two of the uninvited joined with Fiona, who reached across Ray to grab the head of the Council's attention. Alice's spirit lifted with at least two changing their ways. She was not a fan of Joe Smith. He was a certain level of hellraiser that did not get along well with others. Though he worked hard in life, shit never went the way he planned. As a result, he wanted to be left alone. That was what Alice understood about him, and being bothered created turmoil. This time, Joe had a place to direct his wrath.

She made eye contact with Marlene, and the bartender nodded her direction.

"I've already assigned them to Vivian," Marlene said.

She smiled back at Marlene while entering the kitchen. Camila operated the pizza ovens near the door as she decorated the sauce ladened pies. She checked the order counter, verifying if any of her trays were completed. She spotted Chef, who still busied at his tasks but began to speak softer to his crew.

Chef was present the first night she came to Gravedigger's. She never understood it when her husband opened the business all those years ago. Back then, she was unaware of how the place actually ran and didn't realize the stakes until she found the paperwork on her own plot. She came out for a visit, and everything within the building shocked her. From then on, she never wanted to leave.

After she enjoyed what was here, she experienced the best parties ever. Nothing topped that night. Not even the rock concerts she attended all over the world. She married into money, and once she confirmed her husband was screwing around on her, she did whatever she fancied. However, never did she cross the barrier of being with someone's spouse. She did not like it happening to her, nor did she want another to experience it. Marital issues happen, they occur all the time, she did not have to be the cause of them. It was her code. She never expected anyone else to follow it.

Alice appreciated it when someone held a door open for her or smiled as she walked by. The more she aged, the more she valued those experiences. The flip side was the creepy smiles. Those bothered her. The way the sick bastards grinned, and the dead eyes roaming over every part of her body except her face. It was nothing more than staring at a rabid animal waiting to pounce. Occurrences like those were few and far between, but once for anyone was too many. To date, a disturbed soul such as that had yet to enter Gravedigger's. For that, she was thankful.

She worked the business after her husband's death. They had a huge fight about what that meant in the afterlife, and though her husband set her up for an eternity, it did not mean they had to spend it together. Now, he referred to her as his *Ex*. He still walked around as in his mid-fifties. She preferred her twenties. The time when her body still bounced back after children. It amazed her how many of those settled for maintaining their appearance on their last breath. That was not for her. She changed herself regularly to fit her different moods.

Alice worked harder now than she did during her life. She still stopped to have the occasional good time, yet she understood one rule most never found: the more you give to Gravedigger's, the more it gives back.

Members had rules, but they also had abilities. She tested hers and pushed everything to the limit and had been doing so for almost a decade. Plus, it was all at a place she enjoyed. After she handed the reins over to Marlene, she stepped back, offering support, and began to move slower. She welcomed crossing to the other side. It helped to know what it would all be like when the time came. She had that advantage. Her asshole ex had it, and her granddaughter had the same.

The true land owners passed the prophecies along. Those carried through the Krol lineage but were cemented with the creation of Gravedigger's. Very few of her immediate family ever came to visit. She always perceived who came in the daylight and what they said.

Only her dearest ever showed at night. Though generations of Krols resided here.

It was her husband who conceived the Council. He did something right. It was magical. No need for streets of gold here, just a great place to go where everyone knows your name. Even if some were not resting well, they could get it out of their system here. Joe Smith was one and received a ban for a rotation. That man sincerely believed he was cut short of a decent life. When he came back, he learned more about his family and lost his shit. Afterwards, he achieved another ban for two rotations. He rarely showed since then.

Of course, most didn't respect the dead, especially if they were total shits when they were alive. Naturally, no one respected those they did not know, and that was a grave mistake. Here, lying about the deceased was also treated like speaking ill of them. One can say the truth about someone, but don't embellish it. Adding anything is known as lying. All of that led straight to Hell unless the one doling out the sentence had a sense of humor, but nonetheless, it was always bad for the living who crossed the line.

Her concern switched to Marlene for a second, and Alice wondered why her granddaughter did not mention her pregnancy. Alice mused about the possible father, but knowing Marlene, she probably went to the doctor and just had herself fertilized. Then again —she paused for a moment, realizing she had not seen Warren or Bernie in recent weeks. Marlene had been inseparable from them for a few years now. Her musings went from carefree to concerned. She ran out of the kitchen and hoped her small realization was only an assumption, not a reality.

ten – confessions

"And the father is?" Alice asked, grabbing Marlene by the arm and secluding her toward the back bar where they could whisper a discussion.

"What?" Marlene asked.

"You know, who's the baby daddy?"

"I'm not ready to talk about it."

"You better get ready because loudmouth sitting right there will announce it to everyone as soon as he pays attention. It's only a matter of minutes."

"He wouldn't."

"He would." Alice patted Marlene's hand. "I didn't know you were with anyone else other than Warren."

"Bernie."

Alice did not attempt to hide her smile, though she attempted to remain sincere. "You are truly my granddaughter. Are you saying Warren is the father?"

"If it works that way, then yes."

"Have you seen him since you started with symptoms?"

"No. And don't say it like that. It's a pregnancy, not a disease."

"I'm not so sure."

Alice covered her mouth. Her eyes went wide, and she glanced at her ex-husband. He smiled. She shook her head, and suddenly, his toothy grin vanished, almost as if he comprehended what Alice understood.

"What's wrong?" Marlene asked. She worried about the possibility and what it meant for Warren to be the father.

"It's part of the prophecy."

"Prophecy?"

"I didn't think it'd happen anytime soon and definitely not with my own kin."

Fiona motioned for Marlene. Her two friends who had followed Alice earlier were still at the bar and apparently were ready to offer a confession.

"Okay," Marlene said to them.

"I'll grab the pens and paperwork," Alice said as she ducked under the counter, probing for the items.

"Ted and Victoria," Marlene started.

"Vickie."

"For the moment," Marlene said, "you are Victoria. After you sign, then you can go back to being Vickie." The younger woman nodded as

Ted and Fiona stared at Marlene as if waiting for apocalyptic information. "Now, you will sign using the pens we give you. This is a binding agreement. You are not members, not yet. However, the arrangement allows you to return whenever you want, but you can never tell anyone about this place or what happens here. I mean anyone. This includes a priest's confessional all the way to police detectives, court of law, all that. You can never talk about it except here. Otherwise, you end up right back here, and that won't be good for you. Plus, you still have a small debt to pay, but that will be negligible compared to your friends."

Ted and Vickie both nodded as Alice placed two papers in front of the pair. She offered them wooden dip pens.

"Is there ink for the tip?" Vickie asked.

"No need," Alice said.

"Just sign your name," Marlene said. "The tip will take care of the rest. Don't worry if you feel a twinge in your hand or wrist, just sign."

They reached for the pens. As they signed, their hands twitched. Alice smiled as the two slid their papers across the counter to Marlene.

"You two barely made it," Alice said, "and you'll be glad."

eleven – realizations

Ray asked Marlene for a water, as his earlier drinks hit hard and he did not appreciate the fuzziness in his brain. After being in prison and not having any intoxicants for several years, he definitely needed something other than alcohol. He was not bad off but wanted a break before he became inebriated. Though everyone was friendly and this bar seemed like a place he could let loose, he should keep his wits about himself. After the long incarceration, it would be a welcomed opportunity to let his guard down, but he wasn't sure if he was ready for that. He required his edge. Also, the man next to him came off as fairly intelligent, so Ray would have to stay up with the wit. Brainy people who drank, no matter how young or old, tended to drink anyone into a coma. However, besides not wanting to pass out, he at least wanted some great conversation.

Ray turned in his seat, overseeing the action around the bar. Fiona sipped on a lemonade while focusing on her two friends sitting with her. One of the guys from Fiona's old table rose up and headed away from the group. The young man disappeared in the unlit hallway leading to the restrooms.

"That's Daniel," Fiona said in a casual tone. "So, he'll be the first."

"First to what?" Ray asked.

"To get his due."

"From being uninvited?"

Fiona nodded and returned to facing the counter. Marlene brought Ray another water. He kept his focus on the dark entryway. A man in a faded leather long coat and worn cowboy hat entered the area. Ray had not seen this person yet.

"The fireworks are just getting lit," Julian said.

"Joe?" Marlene asked.

"Yep."

Marlene's expression never wavered; she went back to work. Ray wondered if it was really Joe Smith and if someone should assist the younger man in the bathroom catching an ass beating. He had some knowledge of things like that from his recent residence. Restroom beatdown experiences were something to avoid.

"It is," Julian said.

"Is what?" Ray asked. No way that was a dead guy from 1850.

"Read the room, Ray."

Ray searched the faces around him. The diverse people and variations of their fashion did not make sense. It either really was Joe Smith or this was the best performance for a time capsule kind of bar.

"And you shouldn't," Julian said.

"I shouldn't?"

"Think of prison rules, Ray."

The older man pointed, his finger tilting up. A television came on, and it was as if they watched a movie. The scene was the bathroom. Ray recognized it as the bar's. The walls were black, all the porcelain white. Ray could see the sinks within a green cabinet top. The area appeared too clean. It dawned on Ray that he and the males from the group of uninvited were probably the only ones using it.

A man wearing a tan and worn cowboy hat along with blue shirt, beige vest, and long coat walked up behind Daniel. The approach was too close. Daniel had to feel the man's breath on the back of the neck. It made Ray's skin crawl.

"Do you mind?" Daniel asked in an irritated tone.

The sound quality amazed Ray. He glanced around for speakers but located none. The image was clear, and the whole bar became silent. Ray checked the friends' table and saw they stared at a screen across from them. Everyone watched, from what Ray could see, except Fiona.

"Don't mind if I do," the cowboy said in a low, raspy voice. He grabbed Daniel by the back of the head, pushing his face into the wall above the urinal. "Don't wet yourself."

"I won't if you let me go."

"That's not happening, son."

Daniel placed his hands on the wall and pushed back. The cowboy stepped to the side, swiping his foot underneath Daniel's legs. The young man fell backwards.

"Watch your head," the cowboy said as Daniel went down. The cowboy set his foot on Daniel's throat. "You go to get up and I'll stomp your neck. So don't move. Understood?"

Daniel nodded. His eyes never turned from the cowboy's face.

"Good. We need to talk, so I'm gonna letcha up. You go to run or sass me and I'll start thrashin' ya. Understood?"

Daniel nodded again. The cowboy moved his foot, and Daniel stood, brushing himself off.

"The floor is usually cleaner, but when interlopers like yourselves come in, you tend to treat this holy place like any other saloon. So it's a bit nasty."

Ray struggled with imagining any dirt at all existed in there. It looked like a movie set.

Daniel glanced around as if searching for a way out. Joe stood between him and the door. The room only had the one entrance. There was nowhere for Daniel to go even if he tried.

"Now for introductions," the cowboy said. "You're Daniel Maroney, and I'm Joe Smith."

"Sor—" Daniel started, but Joe placed a finger over the younger and smaller man's lips.

"Too late for blubber. Since you said you're my guest, and in order to get this flint fixed, you should know something about me."

Joe took off his hat and smoothed back his hair, returning the headwear to its perch. He allowed a toothy grin with only two missing. His brown eyes sparkled from the glint of light reaching underneath the hat's brim.

"Back when I first settled here, I was poor and lookin' for an opportunity. I was young and thought I would finally settle down and have a family. Can't do that when you don't have prospects. Land was cheap then. Even had some cattle. I worked it for a few years and became known in these parts for havin' good beef and hearty crops. I stayed away from profit crap like cotton. I wasn't tryin' to make a mint, just earn a livin'."

He pointed at Daniel. "You don't know what it's like to go from nothin' to somethin'. All of a sudden, everyone wanted to pair me up with a bride, and I took one. Unfortunately, she died durin' childbirth, along with the kid."

Daniel glanced down at his feet. Joe stood straight, rolled his shoulders, and adjusted his hat.

"I see my story is already borin' the shit out of you," Joe said. "So we'll come back to that later, after I settle with your friends."

"What are you goin—" It was all Daniel got out prior to Joe's gloved fist striking Daniel between the eyes. The young man dropped like a dead bird from the sky. Except Joe caught the younger man before he hit the floor. As Joe held on to Daniel, the cowboy glanced over his shoulder and stared right into the television screen and smiled.

"I'm comin' to rustle up the rest of ya," Joe said.

A commotion erupted as the uninvited scrambled from their table and out the front, all of them pushing and rushing themselves out the door. They left as Joe rounded the corner carrying a knocked-out Daniel. He sat the younger man in a chair and went outside. As he did, he motioned at the television.

"I'm not done yet," Joe said, and exited.

twelve - stragglers

The television scene switched to the parking lot. The uninvited stood stationary. They waved their arms and appeared to attempt to move other parts. They made noises but did not speak. Their feet remained planted. A couple of the young women attempted to talk, but only high-pitched squeals escaped their closed mouths.

Ray glanced at the empty table where they once sat. Alone, Daniel slumped, unconscious, in a chair. His head drooped. Ray figured a few hours would pass before the guy opened his eyes.

"Which one of you is the badass?" Joe asked, pointing at the group.

They stopped all arm motion as their eyes all gave way to Brad. Joe walked over to the biggest one of the bunch. The cowboy studied him.

"Come on, the crops ain't gonna grow without some blood, so who's the badass?"

All eyes were on Joe standing in front of Brad, nose to nose.

"Badass is the correct term," Joe said, "right? For your generation?"

Joe nodded, and Brad followed along.

"Or," Joe continued, "do you call each other the shit. I mean if you are a tough guy, then you are the shit. Or is that a different time?"

Brad shook his head. Joe tapped the young man's forehead three times.

"Don't matter, the shit or badass," Joe said. "I have it on good authority you think you are both, right, Brad? Hard to believe that, since you ran out here to save yourself. Instead of goin' in the bathroom to rescue your buddy."

Joe took several steps back away from the group. Brad was free. He didn't charge at Joe; he took off running further into the parking lot. Before he reached a few steps, he tripped, and Joe was over him in no time. The cowboy plunged his hand into Brad's back, creating a loud *pop*. Ray recognized the sound of breaking bone. Joe removed his blood-covered hand and placed his foot in Brad's back, then he turned to the group.

"Why don't y'all go back inside and enjoy your last meal and drinks."

Ray watched them file in and sit at their table. Daniel didn't stir. They lacked the chitchat and laughter from earlier. Two bouncers made their way to the front of the bar. They were new—at least Ray had not seen them before. Another two perched near the entryway to the patio. Of course, Ray didn't think anyone from the uninvited could run from whatever would happen next.

Meanwhile, Joe spoke to the patrons from the screen: "I'm not done yet." The corners of his mouth twisted up. He focused on Brad, who remained face-first into the parking lot. "I get some of you will say this is extreme, but this guy is a little shit. I have a spot for him to go, so if you're asking me to have a heart, don't mind if I do."

Joe chuckled at his own brand of humor. He bent and returned his hand into Brad's back. It appeared like he was rummaging through a bag, until he stood up holding the heart out for the television. The screens went blank.

Some gasps came for the table where Daniel continued his slumber. The rest of the bar resumed its rumble without their rowdy behavior.

"Well, Ray," Julian said, "this is where I leave you for a time. I have to make my rounds."

"So that's it?" Ray asked, gesturing towards the television. He struggled with why no one wanted to help.

"Marlene and Alice warned them. They saved three. Now, this is the punishment, so there's plenty more."

Like a politician working the fair, Julian went about the floor, talking to others sitting at the tables. He wasn't asking about their service. He was catching up with all of them, their thoughts and ideas.

Ray hoped this was not some weird reenactment type of place, that Joe Smith was actually interred in the graveyard. Because maybe his grandfather might return to the bar. He now understood how his grandfather would know about him showing up for a visit.

thirteen - titles and roles

Alice returned from a table and waited at the corner of the bar. She wanted to confirm with Marlene one more time, but she already had the answer. This would need to be verified. Her eyes drifted to the guest and member books, then to the guests lined up on the stools. Ray glanced her way a couple of times.

"What?" she asked.

"Were you married to Julian?"

"Yes."

"Do you mind if I ask for how long?"

"I do not. Forty years."

"You don't look like you were married for that long."

"That's a benefit to being a member, Ray." She lifted her head and, with both hands, fluffed her hair as he studied his drink. "You either don't believe I'm dead and buried or you have other questions."

Ray licked his lips, sipped some water. "Is it possible for my grandfather to show up here?"

"Of course, but I can only speak for me, what I will and can do. Such as my age appearance, there are side effects when using those."

"Side effects?"

"Yes, it creates certain urges."

"Like what kind?"

"Well, if you lived your life as a nun or priest and kept your vows, then those urges might be sexual in nature. If you lived your life trim and fit, always watching what you eat, never taking in a sweet, then you will probably crave junk food. If you were poor, then you want money. It's different for everyone."

"What are your urges?"

"Me, I played most of my life, so I work."

"Here at the bar."

"That's right, here at the bar."

"But didn't you run this place while you were alive?"

"No, I always had help. I partied. The absolute worst possible manager. Then Marlene came along, and I never really did work after her."

"So Marlene is ..."

"My granddaughter."

Alice waited to see if Ray asked anything else or wanted to add something. Her dearest grandchild walked by, who showed no signs of being pregnant other than a slight glow from her aura. Alice dug deep in her memories, attempting to recall if she could see such things when she was a breathing contributor to society or only as a member of this particular purgatory party.

"Marlene," Alice said, "we need to talk, especially since you-know-who isn't sitting at the bar."

"Okay."

The two went into the kitchen. The staff was in high gear. Mostly cleaning, with some cooking still ongoing. No one paid attention to the two women.

"Are you sure about your relations?" Alice asked.

"Certain. It's only been Warren and Bernie."

"Oh my."

"Oh my what?"

"Nothing. I just need to go out back. Can you get coverage for my tables?"

"Sure."

"Also, Ray was asking questions. Fiona may have overheard some answers."

"I'll check on them."

Alice rushed out the back of the kitchen, and Marlene returned to the bar. There, she poured a pint of Pacifico and almost took a sip. She paused and sat it in front of Ray.

"Thanks," he said.

"How's it going?" Marlene asked her patrons across from her.

fourteen – choices

The music played, and Ray caught on that the volume rose with the crowd noise. Marlene never adjusted the sound system, nor did any of the other servers. There were no DJs either. The digital jukebox hung on a wall, and no one selected any song; the next single always came up. From Blues to Rock to Country to R&B, it was the best collection he ever heard.

The bar appeared crowded. Ray checked on the uninvited. Daniel's body still slumped in the chair. No one at the table spoke. Ray observed Fiona was doing the same as him. Ted and Vickie chatted softly. Finally, one of table group did something by standing and addressing the others.

"I'm not sitting around anymore," he said and walked to the front. He tried to push past the bouncers and did not get far.

It took a second, but Ray remembered the guy as Nick. Though not the gargantuan size of Brad, an obvious gym junkie nonetheless. That type of muscle definition came a little from genetics but mostly from regular working out with heavy weights. His pecs were more pronounced than most women's breasts, and his chiseled arms were very much like any comic book hero.

Joe Smith entered, grabbing the young man by the collar. "You wanna leave?" Joe asked. "Don't mind if I do," and they disappeared through the front.

The television didn't come on for this one. Ray comprehended it wasn't good. He believed Nick's outcome was something similar to Brad's.

Three ladies and Daniel remained by themselves; not even a server approached the table. They weren't looking at one another. All of the ladies' faces tilted downward as if awaiting a sentence. Ray's heart crumbled a bit for their outcomes. It was too severe for just wanting to party, and this place amazed him. Except, this definitely was not a normal roadhouse. However, anything worth a damn always came with sacrifices. Gravedigger's did not hide these.

For his entire life, even prior to incarceration, Ray went with the flow. Prison life contained a lot of what he wanted to forget. Adapting to any situation was his attribute. He loved this venue, though it was somewhat haunted. At least he had an idea of what happened after this life. Though he wondered why he had not seen his grandfather.

Ray checked the time. His watch displayed the same time as it did when he entered the bar at twenty-one minutes before nine. He took some joy in finally getting to wear the Rolex again. It was the last gift from his one true friend, Enzo.

The crowd hummed along, almost every table filled. The packed place carried lively conversations across the joint, with the occasional loud cackle. Ray could not hear the jukebox at this point. Daniel sat up and drank some water. Ray surmised Daniel had a broken nose and a possible concussion. A bouncer walked up to what remained of the uninvited. He directed a finger at the front as Joe entered with another person, who wore a purple hooded cloak. It was all Ray could see of who accompanied Joe.

All conversation stopped, as did the music.

Joe placed his left boot on an empty seat once occupied by others once claiming to be his guests. He hunched over and leered into the group. The cowboy raised up his hat so everyone seated could view his weather-beaten face. An earthy, tobacco aroma wafted from the man and floated through the area. He pointed at Daniel.

"I have a deal for you," Joe said as he inhaled a long drag from a cigar. "If you take me up on my offer, as well as one of these others"— the cowboy waved a hand in the direction of the three women still sitting at the table—"then the other two won't quite end up like the tough guys. Their souls are with Heaven here." Joe gestured at the person next to him.

A buzz stirred throughout the bar. Ray glanced back at Marlene. "Heaven doesn't sound too bad."

"Heaven isn't a place," Marlene said. "It's the being standing next to Joe."

"The young woman?"

"The being. Someone not of our understanding and always appears as something or someone else when walking among us."

Ray faced the direction of the interlopers' table. The murmurs across the floor died down as Joe searched the faces of the four. The cowboy held up his gloved hand with a finger pointing upward to signify he was about to continue his message.

"As you heard earlier, I was married once before; she passed during childbirth. I went through two more brides. Both dying with child. None of this happened right after the other; this was over quite a bit of time, with my remarrying every few years. It never worked out."

Joe stretched his arms and stared back at Daniel. "The seasons go by faster and faster, and finally, a wonderful young woman shows up and offers herself to me. Her parents passed a week earlier, leaving her alone. So through our marriage, I gained her property. It was good business."

He smiled as if in remembrance. "She was beautiful as all get out too. She had wide hips and liked to rut a lot. I mean a bunch." His expression faded as he glanced at the ladies. "Sorry for being so brash. She wanted kids bad, so she'd get me out in the barn, out in the field, and every night at home, along with some mornin's before the rooster crowed. Even when she bled. Hell, I didn't care. It felt the same either way. She tried and tried to make a baby. It didn't happen. Finally, one day, we were going at it and my ticker stopped. Right at the best part too. It took her a second to realize it. Once she did, she cried."

Joe paused and shrugged. "I never figured out if her tears were about me dying and grieved my lack of company or 'cause her security vanished. She's not here, so I never found out."

He lowered his head, almost as if he was praying, then glared at Daniel. "Funny thing about that final round with her; she became with child. She didn't die at childbirth, however, and before she delivered, she was able to hook up with a young preacher while he consoled her about my death. She already knew she was pregnant, but that young preacher didn't know. The dirty bastard, served him right. Raised my kid as his own. That preacher's last name was Maroney."

Joe grimaced. "Any of this ring a bell? And what do you know? A few generations later, you show up. Makin' up stories about me. Wakin' me from my rest."

"Your rest?"

"Yes, my rest. Don't tell me you're stupid too? We can party for eternity here or we can sleep and sometimes mix the two, but when I have to wake and deal with this nonsense, well, that makes me a bit unruly."

"I'm sor—"

"Stop the blubbering. Own it. You lied even though you could've been a guest since we're kin. I was long forgotten until you wanted a beer. So you traded your soul for a pint. Now I want it. I also want my family tree to continue. You are the last child from that lineage. So I have an offer for you."

Daniel maintained eye contact.

"Now, Daniel, I'm gonna set some conditions. You don't have to choose them. You can go on with your friends and be under Heaven's care. You know, the badass and the runt, plus these three."

"Conditions?"

Joe laughed. The cowboy appeared to be giddy. "You're gonna love this. You have to work here."

"Here? I'm a financial trader. I make over a half million a year."

"That explains your pasty pale skin. Besides, under my rules, money is no longer of value for you." Joe jabbed Daniel in the face, hitting the younger man right on the busted nose. Daniel grasped his face and bent over wailing. "Now, young man, show your elder some respect and allow me to finish."

Daniel wailed. His cries echoed across the building.

"Now. Now," Joe said, "be a man and stop that blubber. I only tapped you this time."

Daniel's voice softened, but he still whined. Joe stared down at him with a perturbed expression.

"Can you shush?" Joe asked.

Regina consoled Daniel as he tried to stand up.

"Now, you'll work at the bar and answer to Marlene over there." Joe pointed in Ray's direction. No one turned around to Marlene.

"You change your last name to Smith and you get married." His finger motioned across the group. "Then you have a family. You can live a long healthy life that way. Otherwise, Heaven here has a way with torture."

Daniel nodded. "I'll get married."

"Tonight?"

"Tonight."

"And to my goat?" Joe cackled at this; he enjoyed that line. After about a minute, he settled down and gathered himself. "Just kidding, relax." Joe squared his shoulders and stared at the three women. "Now, I need someone to marry Daniel."

"I'll do it," Regina said.

Joe's brown eyes brightened with the statement. "Funny, I was going to let him pick, but really, you should choose."

"I choose him," Regina followed.

"I do too," Shelley said.

"Too late for you," Joe said, "but lucky enough, I'm in the mood for makin' deals, so I have one more for the two of you." He included Harper in his gesture at Shelley, "Whoever makes it to their ride first …"

Harper jumped from her seat and pushed Shelley down in the process, knocking her friend to the ground as she rushed out the front between the bouncers, who parted ways. Shelley barely stood as Joe smiled at her.

"Stay right there, darlin'," he said. "I'll be back in a moment." Joe dissipated.

Within the bar, the televisions resumed the parking lot broadcast.

Harper stared into the oversized Cadillac SUV as she searched her pockets for keys, then shook her head. She failed to notice Joe standing behind her.

"What I was going to say before you bolted out here was …" he said as he shoved his arm through her back. Between her breasts, a red spot formed as Joe's hand pushed through. "Whoever gets to their ride first wins an all-expense filled eternity to spend with Brad and Nick."

Harper stared wide-eyed at the intrusion going through her chest. She appeared as if she was going to scream, but her body collapsed, yet her soul remained standing in front of Joe. He held her heart to her face.

"Funny thing," he said, "all those modern karate movies where they remove the heart from another fighter, it shows the organ still beating. With you, Brad, and Nick, it never beat. Not once. I think those guys are full of shit … like Brad was."

The screens went off. Joe returned to the table next to Shelley. He wrapped his arm around her, smearing blood on her shoulder.

"You seem like a good one," he said. "We'll sort you out later; just stay on my good side … That means don't be a dumbass."

Ray's own heart broke for her. It was always the fear of not knowing the outcome that bothered him.

fifteen – changes

"Ray," Marlene said, "someone bought you a drink. It's from a member, though you do not have to take it."

"Thanks," Ray said without paying attention to what she served. "A couple of quick questions while I'm figuring a few things out about here. The first, if Joe passed in eighteen fifty, how does he know about karate movies?"

"When a member is buried, everyone sees, knows, understands the memories added to the collective. This is a shared community, so everything you did while alive is known. There are no secrets here, just as there are no lies."

Ray pointed to his drink, which he noticed was different from the others offered at the bar.

"My second … is may I ask who this is from?"

"You may."

Marlene walked away to another well, still grabbing glasses and preparing beverages. The long bar had developed quite the crowd and was as packed as the tables on the floor.

Ray studied the potion she placed in front of him. Everything poured since he stepped foot into the place had been in a transparent container. The pints were see-through as well. They had various beer labels on them, but the contents were easily seen. The dark green snifter in front of him hid the color of the contents, which appeared to match the same shade of the glass. He waved Marlene over.

"Why the different glass?"

"Because it's different than the poison we usually serve."

"Poison?"

"Yes, Ray." She pointed to her hat. "See the skull and cross bones? We serve alcohol. It's a poison to the living."

"And this?"

"It's just a different kind and is sometimes worth the trip."

She smiled and headed down the bar to other customers. Ray glanced around. Fiona spoke quietly to her two friends. Nobody stared at him. No one tipped up a glass to him signifying they'd ordered the drink. No pretty woman with a radiant smile offering a thumbs-up as if she wanted him drunk to take him home. So much for the first day out of prison dreams.

"Well … shit," he said, lifting the glass. He sniffed the drink, and the forgotten scent of his grandmother's herb garden rushed his senses, allowing his mouth to water while taking a long sip. It tasted just like the smell. There was a hint of licorice but bitter. He'd never had anything like it, and his tastebuds erupted, absorbing all of it as he held the swallow in his mouth. He let it roll down the back of his throat, where he felt the burn of alcohol dull his insides. Something else twinged.

His chest tingled as the first gulp settled inside him. He closed his eyes and took a second swig. His body seized on him. He struggled to take the next breath, but the sensation lasted for only a few seconds. When he took his next breath, the air was different. The musky scent carried a distant familiarity. He opened his eyes.

Fear rushed through him. There was no question of what happened next.

He stood in front of a vault. The job conceived by his then-girlfriend. Ray did not worry about himself; this was about Enzo. In seconds, the cops would be rushing him and interrupting this particular safe cracking operation. The guy to his left would sing like a canary. Ray himself would say he was only a hired hand and didn't know any of the guys. He did protect the other on his right, though. Why he was here now was beyond him, but if this was a second chance, then he damned well would do something different.

"Enzo," Ray said, "my sixth sense just went off. You need to go and now. Do it quietly just in case I'm wrong."

Enzo said nothing and disappeared. Ray continued listening through the stethoscope. The borescope indicated where the tumblers were on the other side. He swore he was further along this round when the cops arrived this time. The dumbass to his left this time threw his gun down, and it went off. The officers fired dozens of rounds, hitting the former songbird seven times. No way for the weasel to sing this time around. The cuffs on Ray's wrists still felt the same.

sixteen - verification

Alice walked into the graveyard. She heard a screech owl in the distance, combined with a symphony composed of crickets and frogs. The lone *quok* of a night heron echoed in the tree above her. She relished the slight breeze as she hoped Eleanor was available. Sometimes, that particular spirit transcended to other realms.

The nose bump on the back of her leg signaled her of Tugboat's presence. He trotted through the yard at night. His black coat camouflaged him, allowing him to scare the shit out of the living when they walked through the headstones at night, thus alerting everyone to outsiders. Most of the time, these were family and future members hoping to speak to a loved one. One time, long before she arrived, Tug alerted the sleeping necropolis to grave robbers. Many members still liked to talk about that night.

She never understood why Oliver Bracken gave his spot to his dog, but the man did. So Tug enjoyed being a full member just like the rest. No one ever found out what happened to Oliver, but Tug had been a wonderful addition for more than a hundred years. Tug nudged her again and pointed to her right.

"What's wrong, Tug?"

The large dog whined and trotted over to two trees. An area between them appeared to be darker than the rest of the grounds. The moonlight brightened the red dirt as she approached. They both stepped through the darkened soil.

Some sounds transitioned with her, such as the frog chirps. Additionally, toads croaked and insects buzzed. Her vision adjusted and lightened in the dark. An occasional bubble of a spring erupted, as did flashes of a methane scent. A splash alerted her to the depth of the nearby water. On her first step, her foot slid, sinking into a thick mud.

"Yep, I'm in a swamp," Alice said aloud and shivered.

The black trunked trees were laden with a heavy Spanish moss. Something huge flew past her, then landed on a barren branch a few feet ahead of her. The head spun around to peer at her. Its huge eyes blinked twice. Where the light came from to reflect in such large orbs, Alice wasn't sure, but the beauty of the owl captivated her.

"Hello, Alice," a voice said from behind her.

Alice flinched—some of the old *living* habits never died. She turned to confirm who'd said the words.

"Oh, Eleanor," Alice said, "you're here."

She stared at the elder woman who squatted to pet Tugs. Alice always assumed older, though no wrinkles existed on the face, only white hair, cascading down to where her legs started. The black outfit always worn disappeared in the night. Only her hair, pale face, and hands were seen. Her yellow irises always shined in the night. Just as the owl's did.

A swarm of lightning bugs began to swirl around them. The many random flashes provided a steady light for the duo's discussion.

"Well, you did come to see me, didn't you?"

"I did. Sorry for not letting you know ahead of time. This is urgent."

"About Marlene?"

"Yes."

The wise woman always understood the reason for the visit. Alice appreciated this, since it helped to speed things up. Her meeting settings were all over the map, though the swamp was the most used placed to meet. Once, they met in the courtyard of a castle, still in the dead of night, but it was all lit up like fairgrounds. Except not another soul was there. Alice liked that place the best.

"You want to know about the father?"

Alice nodded.

"Alice, use your words, dear. Sometimes, motions elude me."

"Sorry, yes, I want to confirm that the father is a member in our graveyard."

"Then that means—"

"I know."

The wise woman lifted her hand with the palm up, and a tiny bird landed at her wrist. The purple-feathered creature opened its beak, coughing up two small shells. It took flight as soon as the delivery completed. Eleanor brought her gift underneath her face. She stared for a few seconds, then inhaled through her nose. Eleanor turned to Alice.

"Bernie and Warren are the cocreators," Eleanor said.

"How can that be?"

"You think like you still walk the Earth, as if your heart beats."

"Well, I was that way longer than what I am now."

"You'll need to mature faster, Alice. This type of creation isn't under the physical laws. This happens from love rooted in the spirit."

"But ... Bernice is a woman."

"Bernie, or as you say by the formal name, Bernice, was a woman but is now a spirit like you."

"You're saying I can share my soul with anyone."

"If it is true love, then yes."

Alice recognized there were all kinds of differences between what she was now compared to what she used to be. However, she lacked a guide book. Most everyone was eager to teach something once they figured it out. The resting indigenous did quite a bit of teaching, but it was for basic things, such as how they should work with the land and grow the surrounding woods.

But the baby was a game changer. For all of them.

"What will the child be like?" Alice asked.

"Living and completely human. However, this child and any others from Marlene will have gifts regarding the afterlife. Hence the prophetic title."

"Gifts?"

"Abilities. Very much like it was with those from the ancient times when souls were new. As for the pregnancy, think more like weeks instead of months. It's a supernatural thing. Same goes for childhood. Children with these talents can mature faster."

Alice tried to take this in. It was a tale they all absorbed on entering their resting places, but no one ever spoke about it. The Council damn sure never mentioned it. Julian would need to know something more than Marlene was pregnant. They should have had a plan, and with this happening to Marlene, it was a lot to ask from one soul.

"How did this happen?"

"Well, the making of a child of this stature came from souls sharing emotions. In this case, love. From their genuine exchange of ardor as well as the shared energy, the conception happened. It is also why you can't find Bernie or Warren. They've transcended until the child is born. At some point, their spirits will rejuvenate and return."

Alice fought back some tears. Eleanor was so nonchalant about this, but this situation changed everything.

"I should have taken the bed out of that office … What do we do?"

"Be the best great-grandmother you can, Alice, as well as a grandmother."

seventeen - changes

His rights were never read to him, but they never cared. The familiar feel of a cell gave him some comfort. As he crossed the threshold, his world altered. He entered a different room. The plain beige walls and the concrete floor with a drain in the middle created a whole slaughterhouse vibe. Enzo was there, and a woman he certainly recognized sat tied to a metal chair.

"We hacked her texts," Enzo said. "Her plan was to take your money and run. We have a copy of it all being exchanged with her FBI lover. He's already been dealt with." He pointed to her face. "She's gagged because she won't ever shut up." Enzo handed over a wooden-handled machete. "You know what to do."

Enzo left the room, leaving Ray alone with his former lover. She set him up by encouraging him to perform a risky robbery of a jewelry store. They never did stores or banks. They hit individuals. The environments around those safes were easier to manage. Also, they usually uncovered secrets that earned additional cash.

The retail vault held the overpriced ring she wanted to wear to display their marriage pledge. She pushed for the robbery. He mentioned it to Enzo, and his friend thought it would be a great extra take. Instead, she'd evidently worked to rip him off. The past incarcerated twelve years made this obvious.

The different room, the visions, he was not sure what he was experiencing. It was not quite a dream, but things hadn't happened this way. So … why not have some fun with it. Besides, he believed Enzo. Even when he had been in prison, he heard the tales of his high-flying girl and her new beau, but he never spoke about her betrayal of him.

Apparently, her little law enforcement boyfriend wasn't true blue. His employer figured a few things out once that guy disappeared. After about six years behind bars, Ray let it all go. Except now, this experience presented him with an option. He and Enzo had been close since childhood. Enzo's grandfather ran the whole show. A man who had always been cordial to the both of them and even offered them respect as teenagers. Enzo never had a reason to lie. Not even now.

Ray untied the gag.

"Ray," she said, "how are you out of prison?"

He did not need Enzo's story. Her forked-tongue words were obvious floating over her puffy lips.

"Beverly, does it matter?"

She began to cry. "Don't tell me you believe him. I was set up."

"I fell for a fibbing bitch, and you broke my heart in unimaginable ways. However, you can consider this my get out jail free card. And for the record, your hair looks great."

Ray gripped the wooden handle. He was a safecracker. Enzo used him only for high-powered breaking of uppity people that owed them money. The jewelry place was a distraction and one created by the woman in front of him. All he could think of was how when he rotted in prison, Enzo was needlessly killed. It was her fault. She lied. She lived it. His anger ignited inside of him. The more the thoughts of her betrayal raced through his head, the hotter his emotional fire burned. It raged. He'd never killed anyone before, but now it seemed like the right thing to do.

He held the machete up.

"What are you doing with that?"

"Removing that lying mouth from the rest of your body, and I hope the blade is dull."

She pleaded and begged. Ray swung the blade into the side of her neck. He'd hit a homerun his last time at bat in high school, but connecting with her neck, setting the steel about an inch into her flesh, was a better combination.

She screamed.

The very neck he kissed so many times, touching her soft skin with his lips, being as tender as possible. He pulled the blade away as blood poured out of the wound. It pulsated from the gash, covering her green sweater. He swung again. This one sank two inches more, and her screams stopped.

A slight gurgling sound came from the wheezing neck. He saw her chest moving. Somehow, she still breathed. The next swing embedded in something. He struggled as he pulled, finally releasing the blade with a smacking *plop*. Blood flowed from her body and pooled on the floor around his feet. He didn't care. The poisonous snake needed the head removed, and he took one more swing.

It went completely through. Her head rolled off the side of her shoulder, down her lap, off her knees, and onto the concrete. Her glassy doll-like eyes stared expressionless at him, her once perfect hair tangled and matted with her blood. He kicked her head. It skidded across the room.

Her torso fell forward against the strap holding her lifeless where she sat. He slapped the machete at the rope and cut through on the first swing, sticking the blade into chair. The cord dropped to the floor. The corpse followed it.

As it flopped onto the concrete, the body he once used to hump into the wee hours of the morning blended into the ground below. His work boots evolved into black dress shoes. His jeans became slacks. He was in a crowded room. He recognized Enzo and Mr. Donatello, as in Big Joey Donatello, Enzo's grandfather. No one ever said the "Big" term, though. Street names can sometimes deceive, with his implying being broad shouldered, muscled, or possibly even fat. Except Mr. Donatello was merely tall along with being very narrow and trim. The silk suits and dark glasses completed his stereotype. No matter; when that man walked in a room, he turned heads and commanded respect. Ray loved Mr. Donatello almost as much as his own grandfather.

"Enough chatter," Mr. Donatello said, "we're here for a reason. We're here for family."

Ray realized someone was getting made and wasn't sure how he was still in the room. He searched the group for familiar faces. One of his all-time favorite guys, Tony, stood next to the biggest man Ray had ever seen. The man was huge. He had to be close to eight feet tall.

Frank stood near them as well. Ray didn't realize Frank was a part of the family but saw the blue cross tattoo on the ring finger, signifying Frank achieved the status. Frank wore a pinky ring but no wedding band. Ray wondered what happened to the wife, since divorces didn't happen either.

Maybe he thought wrong in someone being made. He wasn't, and shouldn't be there if someone was receiving such an honor. He never did anything great for the family except the safe cracking, and that was not enough to get in. Sure, he and Enzo were friends, more like brothers. Ray would do anything for Enzo, including going back in time to correct his mess, but that wasn't enough to get in either. He wished all of this was real.

"To Ray Messina," Mr. Donatello said, bringing Ray back to the moment. "He displayed loyalty and respect for family saving Enzo first instead of himself."

The room clapped. Ray struggled to believe this was actually happening. The smells, the murmurs, the room, it all seemed real, but he remembered sitting at Gravedigger's taking a drink. Marlene did mention a trip. If so, then what a hell of a journey.

"Ray," Mr. Donatello said, "come forth."

Ray did. As he reached Enzo's grandfather, Ray extended his hand to greet the elder, who grasped it. Instead of shaking it, Mr. Donatello pulled on Ray's index finger, straightening it out. Nick Puglisi, who Ray thought could very well be the ugliest man alive, took an ice pick and pricked Ray's skin. Mr. Donatello squeezed Ray's finger, allowing the blood to drip on a small portrait of the Virgin Mary. The red fluid tapped her face and gathered below her chin. It soaked into the paper.

Someone lifted the picture, placed it in his hand, and lit it on fire. Ray grasped it.

"You've already been living what is said next," Mr. Donatello said.

Then the whole room spoke the same line as Ray did: "As burns this saint, so will burn my soul. I enter alive and will leave dead."

"Welcome to the family," Mr. Donatello said and kissed either side of his cheeks.

The room erupted. The embraces were firm, and the different aftershaves and colognes, mixed with the smell of cabernet, filled his senses. It happened so fast.

"Ray?"

It was a woman's voice. Everything went dark.

"Ray? You with me?"

He recognized Marlene's slight Texas accent. He was sitting on the familiar feel of the bar stool as it rested beneath him. He opened his eyes. He was back at Gravedigger's.

"There you are," Marlene said. "I didn't want you to miss the wedding."

"Wedding?"

"Yes, you missed a bit after your drink," she said, allowing for an infectious smile. She came around the bar, where she pointed out to the floor.

Daniel and Regina stood centered in the room, where the pushed back furniture created plenty of space. Off to the side, others occupied the remaining tables. Then Ray recognized two men. Mr. Donatello and his grandfather were sitting at one. They offered their glasses up, acknowledging him.

Marlene touched his left hand. "You didn't have that when you came in," she said.

On Ray's ring finger, a tattooed blue cross displayed itself just past his knuckle, the Donatello family sign. He glanced back at the table, but his grandfather and Mr. Donatello were gone. His eyes watered.

"You sure you're okay?" Marlene asked.

"Never better," Ray said.

eighteen – united

"Alrighty," Joe said aloud. "Showtime."

The bar fell silent. All eyes returned to Joe and his remaining band of the uninvited.

"This is a happy time," Joe said. "Heaven is going to unite Daniel and Regina, and Shelley will be both Maid of Honor and Best Man."

A variety of roses and orchids appeared, decorating the walls and furniture throughout the building. More arrangements emerged, such as candles, childhood photographs of the couple, red heart-shaped lollipops, and a printed love song, all around the room.

Heaven circled Regina several times, and with each pass, Regina's clothing changed. In the end, she had a ring of yellow roses woven into her dark hair. A tanned deer hide created the base of her sleeveless dress, showing off her mahogany skin. The length touched her calves. A floral lace accented it, covering her chest to her neck line.

The boots on her feet were modern with no heels and zippered on the inside part of her legs.

"It's simple," Heaven said, touching the short sleeve near Regina's shoulder, "but it's special."

"Thank you," Regina said.

"Now, time for a wedding," Joe said.

The young couple stood in front of Heaven, who pulled back the hood of the cloak, exposing a slim, feminine face with smooth, unblemished skin and black hair dropping down into the clothing. Purple eyes and lips caught Ray a bit off guard, but no one else around the bar reacted in a negative manner. Prominent cheeks along with a pointed nose and chin completed a doll-like appearance.

"You will stand united," Heaven said, grabbing the nearest hands from Regina and Daniel.

Joe clasped his significantly tanned hands around the young couples'. He held theirs up, and Heaven wrapped a brown ribbon from their fingers to their wrists.

"This union lasts beyond the grave. This tie is a forever bond. One that can never be broken by choice, by will, or by any other while on this plane or another."

Def Leppard's "Love Bites" began to play. Ray found it odd the jukebox chose this song for this moment. No one appeared to complain about it, though. The music stopped when Heaven's mouth opened.

"Now," Heaven said with melodic voice, "does anyone object to this union?"

No one offered an objection. The bar remained silent.

"Do all the witnesses confirm this union?" Heaven asked.

Words floated into Ray's head, and he mouthed with the others, in unison, "We confirm."

"I pronounce you together," Heaven said. "Shelley, you may place the rings on their respective fingers."

Shelley moved and placed a band on Regina's finger and one on Daniel's. As the bride released her grip, the ribbon remained wrapped around the other hands and grew longer as she allowed access for the ring. Both pieces of jewelry appeared to be the same to Ray. A plain black band that turned red once fully on. The rings glowed.

"You mean to tell me," Joe said, "you both already loved each other?"

"I didn't know," Daniel said to Regina.

"You were always oblivious to any words I said or anything I did," she said.

"She's always had a crush on you," Shelley said to Daniel.

"Well, I'll be," Joe said. "You always see the damndest things in this place."

"It's good, Joe," Heaven said. "Everything will be Regina's choice moving forward. She will make good on her word, but to the nature of this relationship, she will dictate the terms when it comes to her and the children, once they come. I've granted her a few gifts in regard to Daniel."

"This sounds fun," Regina whispered into Daniel's ear.

"It will be," Heaven said to Regina.

nineteen – understanding

Before Alice asked another question, she was where she'd started at the gate. Her visit came to an end. She had no idea how much time had passed or if it was even the same night. Those details would come to her. For now, it was still dark, which meant Gravedigger's was still open.

Tugs nudged her hand and took off through the graveyard.

"Thanks for the escort," she said after him.

Alice returned through the back and into the kitchen. It was empty and clean. No one worked inside, so she presumed they must be in the bar.

Alice entered through the opening. No one sat at the counter. Everyone was congratulating the couple. She had missed a wedding. The crowd seemed happy.

Then a disturbed feeling began in her chest. Alice had no idea if this was bad or good news. It was a prophecy coming to fruition.

Most members never wanted this day to come, and the fact that the harbinger was Marlene made it cringier.

Her ex approached.

"Hi, Alice," he said, wearing his charming smile. She fell for it when they were alive, but now, it only pissed her off. Except this version appeared to be somewhat genuine. Something she'd forgotten he offered. "You have an announcement?"

"How do you know?"

"It's obvious, and I've known about Marlene since Bernice and Warren transcended."

"Why didn't you say something?"

"Not my place. You confirmed it with Eleanor?"

Alice nodded. "Marlene's baby is the one."

"So once acknowledged, as a rule, it must be announced."

He smiled wide, almost as if he was laughing. There was the shit-eating grin she hated. She struggled to believe she gave that man five children. His expression made her want to scratch her fingernails down the side of his face, and she was glad she never felt a pang of guilt or regret about getting passed around on a tour bus as if she was a joint.

He turned to the patrons.

"Everyone," Julian said, his voice amplified as if he had a loud-speaker—though he spoke gently, the bar carried it. "Alice has an announcement."

"I know this is a happy occasion, but this is by the rules," Alice said.

All murmurs stopped at this point. The crowd, mostly members, from the faces she could see, were all facing her.

"Marlene is pregnant," Alice said.

Everyone cheered. Marlene stared at Alice with a shocked expression, her hand over her mouth. A few hands patted her on her shoulder. Ray mouthed "congrats" at her.

"Bernice Washington and Warren Delgado have been confirmed as creators," Alice finished.

Gasps went throughout the audience. A line formed as Julian grabbed his granddaughter, bringing her to the middle of the bar where Daniel and Regina once stood. This gave room for the crowd to gather around her. The first to appear was Eleanor.

"I was the confirmation for Alice," she said, turning to Marlene, embracing her. "Congratulations."

Many came by and said nothing, offering smiles and acknowledging with a nod. The ones who were able reached for Marlene's belly. With each touch, she felt her insides stir, an ache within her body, a yearning for holding, and love. Some hugged her. If anyone said anything, it was "Congratulations."

After all the residing members left, Alice held Marlene tight, as did Julian. Next, they kissed her cheek. "You'll always have our love, my Mother of the Dead," they said in unison, and left.

Dawn crept on the terrace. All the patrons departed except Ray, Fiona, Shelley, Vickie, and Ted. Marlene assumed the newlyweds were across the street at the house. Gravedigger's had a way of adjusting the old parsonage. They would already have their room. Marlene lacked the details, but she sensed it.

Heaven stopped before her. "I'm excited. I didn't exist during the time of the ancients." The person in front of Marlene bore a genuine smile. "I'm not missing out on this. Anything you ever need, just call on me." With that, the being exited through the kitchen.

Marlene glanced up as the remaining group focused on her. She shrugged. "What?"

"What does Mother of the Dead mean?" Shelley asked.

"That Marlene will be a mother to someone with special gifts," Fiona said. "It also means Marlene may develop a few of these abilities as well."

Fiona walked over to Marlene and touched the bartender's hand. There was a slight *pop*, along with a spark much like static electricity in a dry, cold climate. Marlene embraced the warmth from her hand as it shot through her body. She recalled her initial thought of Fiona being related. Somehow, they were, and she would have to find out how and why.

"Abilities?" Marlene asked.

"Special ones," Fiona answered. "Not those like how you just know orders in the bar. There's a much bigger picture. I think this explains my own urge to come here."

Things were getting a bit too weird, even for Marlene. For her, she wanted a healthy baby. Something normal. But in the back of her mind, when she first started feeling something forming within her, she understood it was different. She shook her head as she stared at Fiona.

"You know I speak the truth," Fiona added.

"We'll see." Marlene sighed and glanced around the group, who were all staring at Fiona and her. She pointed at Ray and went behind the bar, retrieving a packet. "This is the lawyer's stuff. He'll stop by the house early evening to pick up the signed copies. For now, you can stay at the house with the rest of us."

"Is there room?" he asked.

"Always, when you're invited."

Her new friends moved toward her. All the tables were back in place with chairs and benches stacked on top. Ray appeared to be amazed. Marlene walked over to the terrace and closed the doors. The lights inside went out.

"So, what's next?" Vickie asked.

"All I know for sure is we will open again tonight," Marlene replied, "and that I'm pregnant."

— THE END

afterword

Before I go through some specifics about each story, I want to thank a few people. First, Krystal, my partner in everything; together, we've been through many ups and downs. She is my first reader to all I write, and this is significant because she does not read horror. No matter how much I try to convince her, it's a no go. However, she is an avid reader and provides critical feedback.

After going through most of adulthood without truly embracing what I always set out to do, I finally took the necessary steps to grasp my lifelong dream of writing. My family has been very supportive, and I appreciate them very much. Special shoutouts to Mom, Trey, and Renee for all those early reads of the stories within this book.

Lisa Kastner has been my biggest supporter outside of family. Without her, I definitely would not be this far, nor would I have ever found the courage to attempt this collection. She has read much of my work, and her feedback has been invaluable. She was incredibly kind to provide an introduction to this book. Thank you, Lisa.

A couple of more special notes. Lisa Lee Tone for editing this book and her insights on bringing a story to a reader. She is a treasure of a person, as well as a world-class editor. She is one of the best. The cover of this book was created by Lisa Vasquez. She brought Marlene to life and answered so many "how-to" questions from me for this book. She is tireless, patient, and absolutely wonderful. I have an immense appreciation for each of you. Thank you both so much!

I appreciate all the writers who have been supportive of other writers. It really does take a village. I love conventions like KillerCon and festivals such as Ghoulish. I have had the privilege to be able to discuss writing, stories, movies, and so much more with many writers from all over at both events. I've been able to reach out to local writers in Houston, and I love it when there's an opportunity to hang out. They are an open group and quite supportive of one another. They're fabulous.

An extremely huge thank you to all the readers of this book, none of this exists without you. I'm humbled and extremely appreciative you've stuck around this long to read the afterword. Feel free to reach out to me on social media. I'm a reader too and always enjoy discussing all the stories from other writers that capture our imaginations, sharing why we love them, and possibly how much more we want a story to continue. Please remain positive in making comments.

Running with the stories in this collection, I'll start with "Graveyard Game." It was first published online in 2019 by STORGY Kids. I appreciate them for picking my story up. It was only the second submission from when I began to write with a fervent dedication. The world pandemic did them no favors, and their presence online vanished, but they did get me started, and I will be forever appreciative. It would be over three years before another short story of mine entered the world.

Funny thing, Lisa was the name of the protagonist in the story before I met any of the Lisas involved in the creation of this book. This story is one I worked on since my first job out of college. It wasn't a steady or a dedicated work, but I dabbled on it from time to time over the years as I did with other stories.

"Ghosts in the Graveyard" entered the world last September in an anthology called *Children of the Dead Shadow Playground*. The inspiration came from watching my own children play Ghosts in the Graveyard, in the dark, after scout meetings

"Beer in a Bar" was published in November 2022, in a tribute anthology to Bram Stoker called *Dracula's Guests*, published by Hellbound Books. This was only my second story published and the first in print. There are some great vampire stories within the pages of that anthology. I am very grateful to this press.

About "Beer in a Bar," I have several other first drafts of stories which include some of the vampires from Esther's group. I hope to finish more of their stories someday. They have so much to offer from their travels as well as their unique methods.

The bar where the story starts was one I used to complete a day's work at in Seattle. This one was located underground at the hotel. Usually, I finished work and prepared for the next day sitting somewhere in the place while watching a sporting event. The people of Seattle were always great hosts, the downtown area was always a delight, and it is truly a great city.

"The Madhouse" is a story I had written quite a while ago, but I added a bit more to it. Father Paul is a recurring character in many of my stories. In fact, he is mentioned in "Graveyard Game." His possibilities are endless, and he is a featured character in another book I am working on. I hope to have this completed soon, but some other stories are taking precedent.

"Gravedigger's" is completely new and written in the past year. I love Alice, Fiona, Ray, and Marlene and want to continue to see how their stories grow. Through the course of "Gravedigger's," Ray's story came out, as did Alice's. They both had much smaller parts but grew as the story was recorded. How stories come to fruition is my favorite part of writing. I'm always surprised.

Any characters I've been fortunate enough to bring to life always have the possibility of showing up in another story. Take the mafia story coming out in GabaGhoul. During Ray's trip for cleaning up his past, during his induction, there are a couple of characters from "Mr. No-Name" in this realistic dream/journey. Outside of Father Paul, there are no other recurring characters within these pages. However, many stories currently in development do contain some of the characters in this book.

One last bit: Marlene's story is just getting started. I was surprised with how this story ended. I hope to spend a lot more time with Marlene in the future. Plus, as a former road warrior, I think this would have been a place I would have loved to come across in all my travels.

about jerry purdon

Jerry Purdon writes horror and dark fantasy. He has short stories published such as "Vandora" in *Magpie Messenger: Halloween Issue 2024* by Curious Corvid Publishing and "Mr. No-Name" in *GabaGhoul* by October Night's Press. Other works embody poetry published in literary magazines, Grasslands Review and Metropolis. His short story "Monster" will be published in the summer of 2025 in an annual short story anthology by Running Wild Press and the long fiction piece "Bloodlines" in *Incurable: Stories from the World of CURE* anthology in the Fall of 2025.

Jerry spends a fair amount of time grilling and loves an awesome bowl of chili. His favorite activity is to sit in the Madhouse Pub engrossed in a great book along with his favorite companions, Shelby and Cayenne. He resides in Texas and is married to his ideal reader. You can find Jerry on Instagram: jerry.purdon, Bluesky: @purdonjerry.b-sky.social and online at www.jerrypurdon.com.